T4-ADC-918

RANGE WAR

The cattlemen had driven out the Indians with fire and bullets, but, in turn, were now in danger of losing their grazing lands to the sod-busters. These homesteaders, God-fearing folk from far and wide, came into the prairie to plough the rich, black earth, to sow corn and beans, to build houses and barns, and to fence in what had until then been free cattle range.

The sod-busters labored hard, but reaped mainly bitter fruit. They sweated and toiled in the burning sun of day only to be whipped into submission, tortured or slaughtered in the darkness of night, by hired gunmen of the cattle barons who fought ruthlessly to hold by force what they had taken by force.

Then Russ Morgan returned...

RANGE WAR

Lauran Paine

GUNSMOKE

First published Foulsham, 1959

This hardback edition 2000
by Chivers Press
by arrangement with
Golden West Literary Agency

Copyright © 1959 by Lauran Paine in the
British Commonwealth
Copyright © 2000 by Lauran Paine

All rights reserved

ISBN 0 7540 8098 6

British Library Cataloguing in Publication Data available

Printed and bound in Great Britain by
Redwood Books, Trowbridge, Wiltshire

CHAPTER I

The Lord Is A Man Of War!

They were hunting Russ Morgan like they would hunt a wolf. Men storming over the land with the drum-thunder of their horses' hooves shaking the earth in a country so vast and limitless it was a world unto itself. Riding through the night with the half-light shining wickedly off carbine barrels across their saddles, searching for Russ Morgan as they had never hunted a man before. With pine-knot torches for light, they plundered the homes of those likely to give him aid, accosted travellers and sealed off the roads.

They wanted Russ Morgan dead. They wanted to drag his carcass through the town of Cornell and across the range to the threshold of the squatters. They wanted him as a symbol, for he of all the squatters, had fought back against the power of wealth and might.

Russ Morgan was a strong, gaunt youth just over twenty-two years of age. He had an inward air, savage eyes and a mouth made flat from much waiting, much disillusionment and toil since he could remember. A strange young giant with a forcefulness, a quickness which was confidence, and a power which was fearlessness. His long stride and springing step lent him an aura of fierceness, and his tall, sinewy body with its youthful showings, would soon fill out and tower like granite before men.

He had been a lonely child; he would be a lonely man. But where once this loneliness hurt like twice-experienced grief, later it would turn to hate. The kind of hate that destroys men.

A bleak and bitter boy, he would grow to become a deadly man never totally without fire in the grey restlessness of his glance. And as he had been a strange boy to others, so he would grow into a strange man.

And while they hunted him like a rabid wolf with the jingle of their rein-chains and spurs and the whispering creak of their saddles, and the sullen light off their guns, he would out-ride the best of them, fleeing with a wild sobbing to mark his passing. In his mind was the livid-stained etching of four dead men, and one was his father.

The elder Morgan had been as large a man as Russ was, but much heavier; mighty with the power of three men in his shoulders. There was the same fearlessness in both faces and both hearts.

Elder Morgan was a huge man with a deep-rolling voice and eyes that would smile into twenty guns. He was great in the service of the Lord. With only his hands and prayer he could renew life in the dying calf, winnow the blackness from a wild horse's heart, guide the settler's plough across the virgin range of the feudal cattlemen, turning up black ropes of steaming earth that hurt to bear for him.

Those same hands would lie clasped in Sam'l Morgan's lap while he listened to the threats to move on, leave the realm of the cowmen. Russ had heard his answer often enough: "The sheep gone into this new land to find homes and peace and labour for their days and bring forth from their seed others to labour for *their* days—all in the guidance of Christ Jesus."

And they killed him.

They didn't come into his fields and strike him down,

for there was the uncommon greatness of his strength, but they came nevertheless, riding fast on their half-wild horses, never breaking their stride, and sent a rippling slash of gunfire at the big man behind the aged horse. He had stood wide-legged looking after them, both boots planted in the newly-turned black earth, then he crumpled slowly, and Russ had seen it happen from a distance.

That was the picture a gaunt youth carried in his head and would never forget so long as he drew breath. It was particularly vivid when he was out-riding the bands of pursuers, the cowboys steeped in the glory of their trade who had always used guns to uphold the righteousness of the brands they worked for; the right of might and wealth to hold forever the free-ground.

The elder Morgan had come into the land with thin horses, snail-paced oxen, big-eyed children and a worn, weary woman who believed in two things: her man and God, sometimes confusing the one with the other. They had all worked to sow a crop and erect a sod hut, and store quick-growing turnips in a cellar against the cruelty of that first winter. When they were still there the next year, the cowboys had come to harrass, to mock, to laugh, and finally to threaten and kill.

The son remembered those things when he stood over his father, saw the scarlet spread, then stop spreading when death came. Gazing downwards he knew his father had recognised his murderers, for even as far off as they had been, Russ had also recognised them, and he thought how safe they felt now, with the elder Morgan dead, thinking he alone had seen them.

Russ had gone back to the sod hut to face the stare-stillness of his mother and the wild grief which wouldn't be still in the faces of his younger brothers. He had taken down the gun, gone back out, taken the old horse from his plough-bondage and leapt upon his back and rode into the dusk.

He had waited in the trash-littered alley of the cowmen's town fifteen miles southwest of the homestead until the first one came out where his horse was tied.

" Jake Yarbro! "

The rider had seen him and the cocked rifle and stopped dead-still.

" Turn towards me."

" Sure, kid; sure." Yarbro twisted a little and he also crooked his arm. There were two blasts, one a little ahead of the other. Russ knew Yarbro and the others, wild and unruly, as deadly as death itself. When he'd seen the arm bend he'd fired.

Yarbro's horse shied violently, his rider down in the dun-dust, his lips working over words he never uttered.

Then the gangling youth had wheeled his aged horse and ridden down the night until he came to the empire of a man named Saul Bennett; a thick-bodied man with a coldness in him that was a legend. Powerful and entrenched, Bennett owned the cattle upon a thousand hills and his brand, SB, was like a challenge. At SB the kid tied the horse, walked down close and threw a rock against the door of the log bunkhouse and called for Dan Ely.

Ely came with his stilted walk and shoulders thrust forward to meet life head-on, and died with a high cry and a flash of flame.

The old horse tired under the pursuit for the SB had boiled out into the night like hornets. The darkness was Russ Morgan's saviour and he drew aside in it, waiting. There was still another SB man he wanted. He rode slowly after him and called out. The rider drew back, thinking it was another SB man, and fretful that the others were sweeping far ahead in their wild charge down the land.

"Who is it? Come on—dammit—hurry up!"

"It's me," the big youth said. "Russ Morgan. Get off your horse!"

In the match-flare the SB man held rigidly a foot from his cigarette, Russ saw the dumbfounded stare when he cocked the rifle.

"Get down, Belton!"

"Listen, kid—don't be a . . ."

"*Get down!*"

"Sure, kid," Charley Belton said softly, and did the same thing Jake Yarbro had done—and the result was the same. Two slamming explosions, one ahead of the other.

Russ had taken Belton's pistol and shell-belt, lashed them to his middle, then he mounted Belton's SB horse and led the older animal back to the sod-house where his mother sat in the rocker teetering back and forth with only the grinding of the runners on the packed-earth floor to break the hush.

"I brought Jehu back, Mother."

Her eyes had raised and held to him, seeing the gauntness—the willow yet to be an oak—the bigness and the shockle-headedness, the greyness of face and the big gun at his middle, while he held his father's rifle lightly.

"Russ, what have you done?"

The grind and groan of the rocker, a rhythmic, ugly sound, was like grief. "I paid them back," he said, watching her.

"You have done wrong."

"They won't catch me."

"Sinful, Russ—sinful."

He felt rebellion coming up. It had been in him as long as he could remember; rebellion which was a blackness in his soul. Work—labour—study—hear the Good Book; in that order his days had passed. And as always, he waited for the spasm of rebellion to pass; the ache behind his belt to lessen for it was in him to love and obey his parents. He stood there in the night with his guns and his youth and his savage-fierce expression, making a towering picture of vengeance with the shaggy wealth of taffy hair untamed, and the fine features, glowing with a greyness now.

" It wasn't wrong, Mother."

" It *was* wrong," she said tonelessly, the rocker noises making a litany behind the flicker of tallow-candles. " You must not kill. Your father taught you that, Russ. *Thou shalt not kill!* "

His answer came in a ringing tone, yet with pain in it too. " An eye for an eye and a tooth for a tooth. They killed him in the field like a wolf. They've burnt out others and gun-shot their critters ... Killed him in our own field, Mother."

After that she said no more. He stood there with his guns and his appearance of breathlessness, of wildness, a while longer, the hate growing stronger every minute. Hatred and a conviction he had done right.

" Mother; I brought Jehu back. He's in the shed. I fed him but he's tired. Don't let Will or Jim work him tomorrow."

" Your father's fields won't be worked any more, Russ." Then the enormity of it showed in her eyes, a living flame enhanced by the guttering candle-light. " He was such a *good* man, Russ—a good, wonderful man. Now what becomes of us left behind? Of your brothers? They daren't go into the fields now. Oh, Russ—you've brought this to us. You've killed . . ."

" Don't, Mother. I'll be back; I'll come back when I

can. Paw said they were Egyptians tryin' to drive settlers into slavery. Well; don't let 'em—stay here and wait for me, Mother; I'll come back."

She held her fingers interlaced in her lap. They were big-knuckled and red; it wasn't likely such hands could have tenderness in them, but they had it, in great and good measure. She looked up at him again. "You don't understand, Russ. You have brought trouble to all the settlers. You haven't avenged your father, you've brought the fury of the cowmen against all of us. Killing *them* wouldn't bring *him* back, it only means they'll kill others."

There was no answer. It was the truth but in the night he hadn't thought of it and now he knew it wouldn't have mattered if he had. A squatter had fought back, yes, but it hadn't been like that really. A boy had wanted to kill his father's murderers—without thought of consequences —that's how it really was.

He said something about them not leaving, that he would be back, then he rode away on Charley Belton's good SB horse. The mixture of grief and hatred made him more canny than the wisest wolf, more wily than the oldest coyote.

They hunted him and hounded his tracks but they never came up to him. The mighty SB, the fiery Texas Land and Cattle Company, and the P-up-and-down, all banded together to destroy one man whom they never caught. It galled them. They offered a reward for Russ Morgan; five thousand dollars alive, ten thousand dead and delivered. And through the hate and fear in squatter faces was a stony glimmer of triumph for the lanky youth who had out-fought and out-ridden the best fighters and riders of Might and Wealth. But, too, prudence kept the squatters away from the Widow Morgan's place. True, two dozen stalwart men had come over for Sam'l's burial.

Incongruous men with mighty arms and great shoulders, in nondescript clothing and bearing ancient rifles which they handled with self-conscious clumsiness; riding horses with collar marks and shoulder galls. They had done their duty by the graveside and they had ridden back to their sod houses, but they did not return for the blight —the curse—of outlawed Russ Morgan was on the place, and terror was everywhere with its jingling spurs and smooth-black guns.

In the days which followed, crystal clear and yellow with hotness, rich with the music of birds heavy with song, freshly alive with corn seedlings arising from the earth, death came to squatters in their fields and it was rumoured that the cowmen's renewed fury was attributable to one man. The drumroll thunder of horsemen racing past in the dark was a reminder that he had fought back.

Besides his mother, Russ had left behind his two brothers. Jim, eighteen, hot and proud with only a little of his father's preachments in his head, and Will, sixteen, with eyes like a lamb's and a gentle mouth. And there was the mother—Jemima—rocking and steeped in an overwhelming grief that made her more tired than ever, and aged.

She had followed Sam'l along a thorny path without once looking away from him, for he had been a strong man and a handsome one. She had suffered with him and rejoiced with him; borne his sons and suckled them into the image of their father, her idol. And now, in this "land of Phillistines," as he had often called it, she had laid him low.

So the summer spun out its golden legacy and winter came, smoothing out the furrows which were all Sam'l had left them, until every furrow, even the shorter one— the one he had never finished—was patted down by the weight of snow; rounded and enriched and made double fertile by the man-blood in it.

There was little set by and the winter was fierce. It was a scourge and a sore-besetting punishment; a winter of suffering for the widow and the fatherless boys she would not allow far from the house. Hunger drove Jim and Will to learn the wiles of the wolves who came to paw at their father's grave and make aged Jehu quake in his lean-to shed. They learned a lesson in survival, the one eighteen, the other sixteen, and came to early manhood in their souls and bodies, if not altogether in their minds.

They caught wolves and traded pelts for guns and ammunition and more traps, and food. They trapped three bears and swapped the hides for Jehu's hay and ate suety bear meat which put grease under their own skins and around their muscles. They lived out the wrath of Nature as well as many another squatter, and better than some.

When spring returned Jemima Morgan felt a quickening of new life with the running of the sap and the bursting willow buds. There was yet a reason to live; she had buried one and lost another but there were still two who were like flint in their raw scrawniness; tough and determined and like iron; struck into premature manhood by God-sent adversity. She could bow her head and give thanks, confusing the prayer to God with the one to dead Sam'l, yet thankful all the same.

But with spring the blight returned, for new squatters came, some to put down their lives between the rows like Sam'l Morgan had done. Nor was it a rare sight to see red flames heighten the breathless sunsets.

Sod houses wouldn't burn but haystacks would, and the wheat and oats which bent languidly in the heat of hot summer until they looked for all the world like swollen, creamy seas—they burned; so did the tall, whispering corn. Death and ruin, twin gaunt spectres, clattered through the land and those who occasionally fought back either died or moved on.

It was a hushed and dreading land full of misery and throttled hatred, and the Widow Morgan knew it—though not from those who stopped by for few ever did. The stigma of an outlaw son persisted—but she knew all the same that nothing had changed. There were signs: men riding by, glaring, who had once come in numbers to tear apart the bedding and kick in the doors, searching for a memory named Russ Morgan. The Widow Morgan noticed things, felt them almost, heard them in the silent nights. But more practically, when she stood in the shade of her fast-growing patch of seedling fruit trees and looked into the faces of passing emigrants with hope shining in their faces, she knew trouble was coming closer.

Squatters came in the summer, sun-bonneted women minding noisy children in the great stillness. Tall men with broken boots and ragged shirts and gaunt like their animals. The overflow of an empire coming out to put down strong roots; to take up what was rightly theirs. They were coming in a wave to splash up against the wild-riding bulwark of cowmen. There were cowmen who had fought off Indians and renegades by matching ferocity with worse ferocity; who lived by the gun and buried because of it, and who had a fierceness in them which was the wall the emigrants would beat themselves out against.

While the summer grew yellow and limpid and aged, Widow Morgan watched the tenseness mount through hushed nights and flare into fright and worse during the dazzling days. Weeks and months of dread and hatred growing and mounting; rumours of men shot down, of fodder and fields burned, of sod houses gutted, of squatters whipped away with nothing on their backs to break the force of drover-whips. She watched it and thought the new land was a beautiful place, bountiful; enrichened by her man, and she would die before she would leave it. There was *that* to hold her, now and forever.

She struggled to think gentle thoughts about the assassins and once or twice prayed for their salvation, but Will and Jim heard the tales of horror with bitterness and cold anger. It was in their grain, also, to pray, but what they asked was different; they wanted death to join against the cowmen, not always be on their side. And they prayed for Russ to return for another winter was coming and they had not dared go out to work the fields.

But Russ didn't come back that year either. He was far off in a dusty, gritty place called the Plains of Abraham. He led a small band of men and when they holed-up it was at a stage station in Colorado, called Virginia Dale.

Until you saw his face you thought him just another cowboy; another member of the untamed breed who were one with the horses they rode. He was out-sized now. The gauntness was gone and in its place was an awesome strength like his father had had. A breadth of chest and span of shoulders calculated to inspire silence in the roughest saloon.

But his face was different. The eyes were like pale blue stones you sometimes saw in the clear water of mountain streams; wet and as clear as new iron—ten times as hard. There was something strange and sad in the face; in the square thrust of jaw and mouth, caught up and held in bleakness. There was light moving in the depth of every expression, too; the kind of light a fanatic might have.

There was more than the strange face, there was almost a legend about Russ Morgan. Even in Virginia Dale, where killers and outlaws of every kind congregated, he was a man apart and none crossed him. He came years before to learn from them. Having learned he stayed to master them all and had done it. He had mastered the feat of using two guns simultaneously; had learned every trick of pursued and pursuer. He had spoken rarely and then only to ask, to learn, and having learned he left nothing to chance and so became a feared and respected man. He was the equal of any gunman in the West, with guns, fists, wiles, and inwardly, with a solidarity purpose, an urgency the others felt but did not share.

In his twenty-fourth year, he saddled up and rode down out of the hills of Colorado without a word or a backward glance. Those whom he had led upon many a foray, wagged their heads and worried. No man of Morgan's riders had ever been taken. They didn't want to see him leave, but there was that other thing about him—whatever it was—and maybe now he was going down to attend to it, then he would return. They consoled themselves with that because they feared to call out and ask.

He rode southward down through the tumbled jaggedness of northern Colorado. It was hot; a burning sun was over him and yellow dust lifted from his tracks, settled over his face and shoulders. The summer twilights were long and clothed in a saffron light that painted him bronze. He made his way slowly, cut out and around settlements and paralleled the stage road, but never rode upon it except for short distances where he could see in both directions for a long way. It was habit; part of the schooling he had set himself to learn well. How to fight fire with fire. He had learned well, for travelling without great haste yet over hundreds of miles, he saw but was not seen.

Memories returned, the past slowly quickened to life.

He remembered his mother's grey face that day he'd walked past her to take down the rifle. He saw the white, contorted faces of his brothers the day "they" had downed his father. He felt the heavy burden he had been forced to leave behind, and a major portion of which lay with a blackness upon his soul. And he felt hatred...

He rode, waiting out the eternity it seemed to take for him to get down to the flatland where swift-running grass bent before the palm of breezes. And down there the sun was even hotter, and for all its beauty it wasn't a tame land, with its challenging distances and scudding banks of summer clouds frayed and heavy; with its horizon where land and sky met, But he wasn't a tame man, either.

He made his camp where hills hunkered low against the shoulder of prairie, back among the scrub-oaks and buckbrush. From there he made excursions in the dusk and before dawn, familiarising himself, finding that what changes had occurred consisted mostly of ruined, deserted sod houses, fields returning to the tangled profusion of natural covert. He rode with a stillness in him to match the hush of the land. Quietly he appraised the men he saw from distances, the big ranches and the remaining squatter hovels. He noted all changes and remembered the things which had remained constant, like his mother's sod house and her little orchard, planted from slips which had grown enough to cast shadows on the deep soil.

Through those first days back, pain and leashed ferocity showed in his eyes—ice over ferment—and in the manner of all men much alone, he talked softly to the big-muscled horse he rode.

Satisfied, finally, that there was no yard of range and upland he wasn't familiar with, he moved his camp to the spongy rankness of a marshy place where there was a matted tangle of feed in great abundance for his horse,

B

and a formidable tumble of limbs and trees, creepers and vines of all kinds to hide both man and animal.

It was a large slough. There was room for an army in there. The horse wrinkled his nose at the death-stench of the place, layers-deep in rotting vegetation. To Russ the gloom and the smell—and the complete lack of horse tracks—were safety; men did not ride in there.

Establishing his camp he thought of the squatters he'd seen riding along the dusty roads, fearful men who saw nothing to a tree but a place from which to hang men. And the cowmen; he'd watched them too. They were centaurs splaying down the night; turning red and seeming to dance before the rush of flames from haystacks. and burning wagons. He had seen something else, too: gunmen. Wealth and Might had brought in paid killers to aid in stemming the tide of empire. That was important to know for it showed that the cowmen were more determined than ever. Resistance could no longer be successful without leadership, without guns as fast, as deadly and fearless, as hired guns would be.

Although he planned carefully, events thwarted him the night he rode out and saw a pillar of fire scrabbling with sharp fingers upwards into the velvet darkness. With his certain knowledge how the cowmen worked, cold with fury, he rode towards it. An old wagon was limned against the brightness which sprang from its warped old frame, and the bows from which hung shreds of burning canvas looked stark, like exposed ribs of some dying beast. He halted in the blackness beyond the raging redness, watching.

Close to the soddy were two riders holding three horses. Russ dismounted and went forward; their backs were to him. In the fire's gushing breath the sound of his coming was lost. He attacked them both without warning. After a moment only the giant with a heaving chest remained upright in the angry flamelight, his eyes dry and his mouth a slit, more savage-appearing than any Indian.

He went to the soddy and shouldered through the narrow doorway, filling it so that his shadow was huge. One gun was dangling, cocked, from his fist.

There was an older man and a worn-out woman and two children at bay before a narrow-hipped horseman who twisted towards Russ's shadow in an annoyed way. Amazement spread slowly over the rider's features when he saw the newcomer wasn't one of his friends. The rider had a coiled drover's whip in his hands. He held it loosely, like a big snake. There was no question of why he held it.

When Russ spoke he noted the rider's black and ferral eyes. " What are you doing here ? "

The black eyes clove to the iron-blue ones. The voice was menacing. " I'm Jess Fuller of the Texas Land and Cattle Company. 'You want to know any more ? "

Russ stepped through the door. " I'm Russ Morgan," he said in the same way. " Do *you* want to know any more ! "

Fuller's venomous stare brightened. He studied the larger man without fear. " You're either a liar," he said, " or you're worth ten thousand dollars dead."

" But you aren't worth the sweat off a man's brow, Fuller. Put your hands out in front of you, Fuller, and don't expect help from your friends."

Fuller obeyed slowly, but he obeyed. There was no longer a shred of doubt in him that he faced the most wanted man in the country. The squatter, his haggard wife and children, were rigid with terror. Inside the cabin was a moving red glow from the burning wagon.

Russ moved around Fuller, flung away the cowman's

gun and looked at the squatter. " What's your name, stranger? "

" Franklin Minot; we're from Ohio."

" Mister Minot, send your family back to bed and come out into the yard." He turned away. " Fuller, go outside and take your whip with you."

Fuller walked stiffly out into the saffron night and held his whip with its blood-stiff snapper. He stopped when he saw his unconscious companions, and stood wide-legged and baleful, waiting. Franklin Minot's gaunt frame was scarecrow-looking in the vagary of firelight. His eyes were glazed with terror and wonder.

" Fuller," Russ said, " you're going to carry back word of what happened at the Minot place to your friends—then you're going to leave the country and never come back. If I ever see you again I'll kill you. If I hear you haven't left I'll hunt you down like a calf-killing cougar. Do you understand? "

Fuller did not reply. His dark eyes were deathly still and the great whip lay in his grip like it was part of him. He was an image struck in the shape of evil and power. Russ jerked his head at Minot.

" Fetch a pail of water and douse his friends. I'll want them standing up." When Minot shuffled away Russ spoke again to Jess Fuller. " When you get back tell your bosses Russ Morgan is back. Tell them he says the squatters've got more right here than they have and I'm here to make it so."

Minot returned with the water, poured it diffidently over the Texas Company's riders until they both groaned and made dust squirt out around them as they tried to get up. Upright, swaying, each felt for the guns which weren't there and blinked whitely at towering Russ Morgan, who handed Minot his gun.

"Watch them; use the gun if they try to run. All right, Fuller, you have a whip; use it. It'll make up for the difference between us." He moved closer. "*Use it!*"

Jess Fuller swung it because he had fully intended to. It made a whistling sound, its dark length cleaving the gloom in dark fury. Russ drew back, but not fast enough. It bit into his corded muscles like all the claws of torment. Fuller knew how to use a drover's whip better than any man Russ had ever seen. Before the lash recoiled he had it in the air again. Three times he cut Russ with it, drawing blood each time, and the last time Jess Fuller smiled. His teeth were square and white in the moving light.

Russ drove forward to get beneath the writhing rawhide. In the face of his charge Fuller still smiled. He reversed the whip and struck downwards with the loaded handle. Russ saw the blow coming, too late. The butt caught him a staggering jolt beside the head, down his cheek and half buried itself in the bulge of his shoulder. Agony flamed out along his nerves. He struck Jess Fuller in the chest. From twelve feet away Franklin Minot heard the crunching blow. Fuller made a high damp sound, like a sob or a cough and his arms sagged. Russ worked into him with a ferocity no defence could stand against.

Jess Fuller did the best he could but he was a gunfighter not a hand-fighter. His best was not good enough, but he wouldn't go down. Russ rocked him with a solid blast to the mouth, another to the mid-riff, and when Fuller bent over, Russ straightened him up with a looping blow. Then Fuller went down.

Minot was the colour of ashes. The Texas Company men were like stone; one of them let out a sibilant gust of breath. Russ stood over the fallen man, sucking in warm night air, nostrils expanded against the inward pull. A moment later, he picked up the whip, coiled it and looked at the two riders.

" How many has Fuller used this thing on? "

They didn't answer. He moved across the yard towards them. The smell of his sweat was copper-like. He touched the younger of the riders with the whip-handle. " Answer me! "

" I don't know." The words squirted out. " I only hired out to the Company a month back. I honest-to-God don't know."

Russ looked at the other man. He was older, harder looking and dried up. His face was seamed, the eyes hot and hostile. " You know," Russ said, " you're an old hand. How many? "

The older man gave Russ stare for stare, but for all his dredged-up courage, he was pale and shaken. " No one knows a thing like that," he said.

" How many times have you ridden out with Fuller? "

" Six times."

" What's your name? "

" Tull Barker."

" Barker; what did Fuller do the times you rode with him? "

" He done what he was hired to do. He burnt 'em out and he whipped 'em out."

" And he shot them out," Russ said.

Barker kept his glance level, but didn't speak.

Russ turned, glanced down at Jess Fuller a moment, then wagged his head. " You two go over and lift him up. Hold him between you."

They obeyed and grunted under Fuller's weight. They held him up with his knees bent because Fuller was taller than either of them. Russ raised the drover's whip, hefted it. Franklin Minot made a gasping protest. Without speaking Russ pointed to the burnt wagon. " Multiply what nearly happened to you tonight, six times."

Each time the whip came down Fuller's supporters staggered and cursed. The sixth time Russ threw the whip down. " Take him with you," he said, " and start walking. Don't stop and don't either of you ever come back to this homestead. And remember this: You wanted to fight—now you've got someone who'll fight back. I'll remember all three of you, and if you see me again you'd better shoot straight the first time, because I aim to kill." He motioned them to go. They did so, unarmed and afoot, struggling with their inert burden.

Russ went to their horses, made the reins fast to the saddlehorns so they could not get their heads down to graze, and slapped them. The animals raced away through the darkness with heads up and stirrups flapping. Distantly, a loud curse floated back to where he stood in the dying firelight with the guns of the Texas Company men in the dust at his feet.

Finally he swung back to Franklin Minot. " I don't think they'll come back," he said, walking closer, reaching for his gun. " If they do they'll regret it even more."

The squatter's face was masked with fear. " I knew your father," he said. " I stood over his graveside ... He wouldn't have done that."

It was like a splash of cold water. Russ stiffened, staring at the older man. He couldn't recall Minot, but that didn't matter. Clenching his fists Russ said, " I'm not like my father in a lot of ways. Look at your wagon, your haystack. They would have burnt you out and whipped you off; you and your wife and kids. How else do you fight men like that, Minot? "

" Not like that. Not like a cougar pulling down a colt. Not like an Injun with a scalping knife."

" You fight fire with fire, Minot. They built this fire;

the squatters've got to put it out with more fire."

"No," Minot said quickly. "They took it out on all of us when you killed your father's killer. For what you done here tonight they'll make a dozen families pay. That's not the right way to fight them."

"What is the right way?"

"Through the law and God's will."

"The law!" He spat it out. "What law—the cowman's law?" His mouth closed with a hard finality. God's will; his father had said that, his mother had bowed to it many times. Now Minot. He turned and went to his horse, mounted and wheeled away. He rode towards the slough with fierce indignation in his heart. There was something in the heavy silence that abetted his mood.

At the slough he hesitated, thinking; then, while the darkness still prevailed, he swung northeast and headed for the distant village of Houton Creek, a settler-town where emigrants were welcomed, contrary to the sentiments in the cowmen's town of Cornell.

Before dawn, travelling along the dusty roadway and almost within sight of the lights of Houton Creek, he came upon a stalled buggy and would have passed on by except for the voice that hailed him.

CHAPTER 2

Life Is The Weaving Of The Wind

"Would you help me here, please?"

He reined up and gazed down at her. She was pretty, but more than that, there was strength in her face. It showed in her fearless gaze, in the set of round shoulders and in the way she stood there.

"The tyre came off the wheel." A gesture indicated which wheel. "The hot weather must have shrunk the rim and spokes. I've been trying to find some water to soak it in."

He knew there was no water closer than Houton Creek. Dismounting, without looking at her again, he noticed the horse between the shafts was drowsing, as though he had been standing there a long time. The tyre was still on, but just barely. Without speaking, he grasped the hub, lifted, eased the tyre back over the wheel and set the buggy down.

"I have this," she said, holding out a tangled coil of wire. He took it and looked once more into her face. There was a barely discernible sprinkling of freckles over the bridge of her nose. In the pale light they made her appear younger than he guessed her to be. Without speaking he wired the tyre into place while she watched.

"Are you a rider around here?"

He said, "No," in such a way as to discourage further questions, but she didn't remain silent long.

"I'm Diane Enright." It seemed to her as though he stiffened a little, but the light was deceiving.

"Enright? I used to know a man named Enright."

"It's a common name," she said.

"This Enright was foreman for the Texas Land and Cattle Company a few years back."

"That's my father," she said. "Only he's a partner in the Company now."

He finished with the wheel and straightened up. There was a bleakness to his expression when he turned, which surprised her.

"That's the same man," he said. "Forge Enright. I didn't know he had a daughter."

She saw shadows moving in the background of his eyes

and thought it possible he was a rider her father had fired sometime. The Texas Company was large and its turnover among cowboys was great. She also thought, from his size and look, he would make a good enemy if he didn't like someone. Without speaking she got into the buggy, picked up the lines and looked over at him sombrely.

"Thank you very much."

"I met three Texas Company riders tonight," he said, as though she had not spoken. "One was named Jess Fuller."

"I know him."

"You wouldn't know him now, and I don't think you'll know him much longer either. I rawhided him with his own whip for burning out a settler."

A shocked silence held her briefly. Far back in her mind something was warning her against this big man. She had noted the two guns which, in a land where a rare few men wore more than one, was like advertising.

"I gave Fuller's friends a message to carry back to your paw, but just in case they don't, you can tell him. Say that Russ Morgan is back, Miss Enright. Tell him a squatter's son has come back to give the cowmen all the fight they want."

He went to his horse and swung up. He sat there gazing down at her a moment, then lifted his reins.

"Wait."

He hesitated, lowered the reins and watched her face. It reflected a little of the inner turmoil. The Russ Morgan legend was known to her, like it was to everyone else on both sides. She was a little awed to be sitting there looking up at him. He had always seemed remote, a fantasy to her; something ghostly and not altogether unromantic.

"How can you be Russ Morgan? He's been gone several years."

"I'm not trying to convince you, lady," he said. "What you believe doesn't matter. Just pass the word along to your paw." He was lifting the reins again.

"All right," she said swiftly. "If you *are*—if you fought with Jess Fuller—then you certainly aren't very smart." Catching his glance, holding it, she went on. "What can one man do against three large cow outfits?"

"Who said I was alone?"

"You are now, aren't you? If you'd just been in a fight with cowmen and had friends, they'd be with you now, wouldn't they?"

"Maybe," he said. "Maybe not. I might just like doing this alone. On the other hand maybe things came up before I got the squatters organised to help."

"Squatters wouldn't help. They won't even help themselves, Mister Morgan."

"You know how it is, don't you," he said coldly. "The same heart's in you as is in your paw. All right, Miss Enright; I won't fight a woman, but I know how to humble them without ever going near them."

"Oh?"

"In your case it would be simple. I remember when your mother died. I reckon that was hard on you. Maybe standing over your father's graveside would be harder— you're older now and he's all you've got left."

She shook her head at him. "You'll never get that far, Mister Morgan. The Texas Company, the SB, and the P-up-and-down, will all be after you like they were before. You don't stand a chance."

He made no reply, but the saturnine expression was more eloquent than words anyway.

"Two guns aren't enough, and they are all you have to

depend upon, Mister Morgan." She paused: "If you *are* Russ Morgan."

"Don't doubt that," he said, "and don't expect me to rely altogether on the squatters. Where I've been the last few years I have friends."

"You mean you'd import gunmen? You're talking like you mean to start a range war. If you do, don't forget one thing—those who will suffer the most will be the squatters."

He smiled like a lion, down at her. "Don't make any big bets on that, lady, and besides, what could happen to the squatters that your people haven't already done to them? They can't do any worse than they've been doing for years. Another thing, if I called in a few friends, believe me ma'm, they know more ways to make your people grunt than your people know."

"If you fight—"

"*If* I fight. Miss Enright, I *am* fighting. It started tonight with Fuller. That was the first fight—and it wasn't much of a fight at that; not the kind I'm used to."

For a long moment she was silent, studying his face, then she leaned forward a little. "I am just as convinced you'll be killed as you are that you won't be, but Mister Morgan, whether you are or not won't settle anything. Why must there be a fight at all? Can't things—?"

"Miss Enright; would your father be willing to allow settlers to take up land here?" He didn't wait for the answer. "Of course he won't. Neither will P-up-and-down or SB. Talk won't settle what's in people's minds. Even if you and I wanted to stop the trouble we couldn't because your kind is against settlers and the settlers will keep coming like the rains. Something's got to give, lady; that's why I'm back—to make cussed sure it isn't the squatters."

"But your interest isn't the same."

"No? I could show you a grave. My father's in it. He got shot down without a chance."

He left her sitting in the brightening murk of a new day and pushed on towards Houton Creek.

Diane sat perfectly still, watching until he was lost to view. A strange feeling of coldness swept over her. She wanted to disbelieve—to think he was just a big-mouthed cowboy—but it wouldn't jell like that, not when she pictured the bitter eyes and two guns; the great hulk of him which bore out what she'd heard of Russ Morgan, " a big feller as strong as an ox."

Finally she slapped the lines against the dashboard and the horse began plodding towards Houton Creek. The wired tyre held although the wheel wobbled erratically.

At Houton Creek, Russ put up his horse and hired a room at the Great Western Hotel, bedded down and slept profoundly. Noises from men and animals drifted in and out of his awareness. In a troubled, subconscious way his mind picked at the happenings at Franklin Minot's place and unbeknown to Russ Morgan, sleeping away most of the day, those same occurrences were electrifying the countryside.

The cowmen were no less stunned than the squatters were. Word travelled fast and by noon Houton Creek citizens had heard of Russ Morgan's return and Jess Fuller's whipping. Opinion, as always, was sharply divided. Generally, since Houton Creek was the squatter headquarters, as opposed to the cowmen's town of Cornell, there was grim and outspoken approval.

In Cornell there was wrath and denunciation, but in one thing both towns were alike; they were excited and agitated by the return of outlawed Russ Morgan, and the suddenness as well as the fury of his attack upon three riders for the cow outfits. In both places there was agitation, and not a little trepedation.

Only Russ himself seemed unruffled. He lingered in Cornell and two days after his fight with Fuller, rode southward once more, laden with provisions for his camp in the slough. He thought it likely that very soon now the cowmen would retaliate, if they intended to, and he had no doubts about that. It was early evening of the third day that he rode southeast from the slough with lengthening shadows for companions, sunk in thought. He had a strategy, and striking again while the confusion was at its height was part of it.

Because he had learnt his trade so well on the Plains of Abraham, he rustled a small herd of select two-year-old steers from under the nose of an SB crew, drove them into the hills and left them there, too footsore to walk back, then he returned to his camp and loafed another couple of days.

The ensuing uproar was even worse than it had been after the affair at the Minot place.

Then he raided a Texas Company's roundup station, selected the best animals, drove them into his swamp, hobbled them there and pushed the rest of the horses for two blistering days until he found a man who would buy rustled horses and take them still farther northward.

Returning, Russ was as wary as a buck-Indian. He rested for a few days and never once, when he rode out reconnoitering, did he fail to see groups of riders crisscrossing the prairie.

He alternated his mounts and cared for them tenderly. Only through them was his life safe. Then he began riding the nights again. The moon, no ally, made him lie over briefly for a few days of the first month.

Part of the fury of the cowmen was based on how

Morgan made a habit of whipping every rider he found with a drover-whip in his hand or tied to his saddle. The most humiliating thing he did was to rob every cowman he met. Usually this included setting the victim afoot; too frequently it also meant degrading the cowmen by forcing them to leave their boots and trousers behind, making them as ridiculous as possible in the eyes of the squatters and their own people.

As the weeks wore on it became increasingly difficult for the cow outfits to hire riders. Gunmen they could hire easily enough, but, aside from the fact that professional gunmen came high, they would not, as a general rule, live in the cow camps nor help work the livestock.

Unrest also seethed among the squatters. Many said Russ Morgan should not be protected; that he was only going to get killed sooner or later and when that happened anyone thought to have aided him would get a bullet in the back. A daring few younger men let it be known they wanted to ride with Morgan. The seeds sown by Russ were bearing fierce and divergent fruit. There was a whirlwind in the making and while it blew, first one way then the other, Russ rode like a ghost, striking often and ruthlessly.

His deeds were slow to inspire the squatters, for although many secretly revelled in his successes, they nevertheless clung to the belief he could not last long, not against Might and Wealth, which was Power. Only the hot-heads among them thought it likely he would go on eluding pursuit.

Meanwhile, Russ employed all the craftiness which had made him renowned in the high country, and avoided the constant posses—the night-riding hunters with their naked guns and pine-knot torches—while continuing to plunder the cowmen's camps, fire their hay fields, stampede their horses and scatter their cattle.

There were other repercussions also. It was one thing to pay for Jess Fuller's five weeks' hospitalization, only to have him saddle up in the night and ride off into oblivion, and quite another to try and replace him, and to replace the others who lit out before, and after, Fuller had gone. Other factors which arose to harrass the cowmen were the unprecedented high cost of real gunmen, and the additional expense of having to hire more men, in order to maintain a constant guard over their remudas and herds.

It was war to the hilt and finally the cattlemen met to discuss it. Saul Bennett of the SB, Hewton Muller of P-up-and-down, and Forge Enright, of the Texas Land and Cattle Company. They met in the poker room of the Cattlemen's Club Saloon. Hewton Muller put it into words when he told them: "It isn't a matter of cost. He's got to be killed. I'm here to say it straight out; unless Morgan is used up, every damned squatter in the country will be taking to night-riding. P-up-and-down will start the ball rolling with a thousand dollars. If that isn't enough, why then I'll match any of the rest of you, but remember this—make the reward big enough, and somebody'll kill him for it; maybe even a squatter."

Saul Bennett sat hunched forward, one arm on the table, his face pressed out of shape by the hand he was holding to his cheek. His pale eyes moved swiftly and there was nothing but hardness in them. "You aren't paintin' the full picture," he said to Muller. "You say if we make the reward big enough one of his own people'll kill him for it. That's bunk; he's had ten thousand on him for almost three years. Anybody brought us his head yet?"

Muller leaned back in silence while Bennett straightened up, rapped the table with his fingers and looked at his companions. "Nope; that reward business failed. Now we got to hire the best gunmen in the West. We got to put more men on the range and hound Morgan till he drops. Listen; those grangers used to hate him because every time he hit us, we hit them worse. Now it's changed; he's everywhere. We send out riders to burn out a squatter and while they're gone he sneaks in and burns our own bunkhouses, runs off our horses."

"And maybe it isn't always Morgan," Muller said. "Maybe he's got those damned sod-heads doing his work too; maybe he's talked them into—"

"That's what I'm saying. They used to hate him, now they think he's great—a real leader. Well; I'm going to say this, and you boys remember it: If we don't stop him damned soon, nothing on earth is going to keep those sod-busters from riding right over the top of us."

Forge Enright puffed smoke out around the stem of his pipe. Up to now he had said nothing. By nature he was a man who thought inwardly and listened hard, but rarely spoke; of them all he was by far the hardest and smartest. "Yes it will," he said. "Something will stop them from riding over us—money. We've got it and they haven't."

"Money hell," Bennett said shortly. "We can break ourselves hiring high-priced gunmen. What we got to do is get him, and get him right soon—within the next few days; within a week or such a matter. I'm in favour of hiring gunmen, don't misunderstand me on that, only I say we can spend a lot of money without getting something worthwhile if we don't watch ourselves." Bennett slapped the table with a broad hand. "What've the gunmen we already got done so far?"

"All right," Enright said, "let's hear your idea."

"Double the reward." At the twin looks of astonishment he nodded vigorously. "Here's how I look at it.

We're spending half that much every month in replacements—horses, riders, rustled critters—and getting nothing but more of the same. Double the reward and some dollar-greedy granger'll blow out his brains from behind. Sure it'll hurt when we got to pay up, but for my share, I'll be glad to fork over—when I see his head at my feet." Bennett peered at Newton Muller. " Now you know why I laughed at your lousy thousand dollars. It's going to take a hell of a lot more than one—or ten—thousand."

Muller was frowning at the tabletop. "That's big money," he said. " I never heard of such a reward before."

" Seven, eight thousand apiece," Bennett said. " Wouldn't it be better to pay that once, than go on paying that much every couple of months in other ways —ways that Morgan's making us pay out, now? "

Forge Enright was smiling. " Bennett," he said, " you always did go overboard. Take a little chew until you've got the taste, then take a bigger one."

" What do you mean? "

" 'You ever figure it might be a cussed sight cheaper to buy this feller out? "

Muller raised his eyes to Enright's face. Bennet said nothing. The older man removed his pipe, cradled it in his hand. " Get Morgan where we can talk to him," he said. " Offer him the reward—ten thousand—to take his loot and get out of the country. If it doesn't work, offer him the twenty thousand, but try the smaller figure first."

" What about the others? " Muller asked.

Enright grunted. " Without Morgan they're so many sheep; you ought to know that by now. Not only that, but without Morgan they'll be easy to convince they ought to move on—to stay out of here. When you disillusion a man you take his heart out. After Morgan's gone and while we've still got the extra hands we can have one night of housecleaning that'll scare squatters off the range forever."

"I don't like this," Saul Bennett said. "I don't like to buy off a damned renegade."

"If I recollect right," Enright said mildly, "you didn't like to cough up your share of the first reward, either, but now you want to double it, because you know what's going to happen if Morgan isn't buried right soon." He arose, knocked out his pipe on a boothell, and said, "Well; I'm going. Let me know what you decide."

The decision wasn't long in abeyance. Russ Morgan hit the holding grounds of the Texas Company one night ten days later and Forge Enright made the long trip to Hewton Muller's place, secured Muller's agreement to go along, then rode to Bennett's ranch and pushed his long legs under Bennett's supper table and ate as methodically as he did everything else.

"The Company's had enough, Saul. It wants action. Muller's coming in; how about you?"

"Coming in—how?"

"We'll have a talk with Morgan. Offer him twenty thousand to saddle up and never come back."

"What's my share?"

"The Company put up seven thousand; your share is the same."

"What? How much did Muller put in?"

"Six thousand."

Bennett reddened and swore and Forge Enright smiled at him. "You knew he'd do that so save your breath. 'You coming along or not?"

"What happens if I don't?"

Enright fished for his pipe and filled it before he spoke. He tilted a candle, sucked in flame with a moist sound.

"You will," he said.

Bennett leaned back from the table, balled up his fists and stared at them. "Yeah," he said, "I will. Will twenty thousand do it?"

"Should."

"How do we work it?"

"You and I'll go see him. Muller says he won't go. We'll send out word we want to talk. If I got him figured right he'll see us."

"Where?"

Enright's hard, thoughtful glance held to Bennett's heavy face a moment before he answered. "If I knew that," he said caustically, "I'd send out a gunman and save us the money." He sucked on the pipe a moment longer. "We'll let Morgan set the time and place, otherwise he's going to be suspicious of us. After that—we make the offer."

"And if he turns it down?"

"I've thought about that. If he turns it down we'll have to do it our way. Do it like you suggested; offer such a big reward some squatter'll blow his brains out from behind. Maybe that'll cost more'n twenty thousand, too, but one thing I'm plumb sure of—the Company's out to get rid of Morgan one way or another—and that's what it's going to do."

Bennett got up and pushed fisted hands deep into his pockets and stalked up and down. "Muller'll suck back again if we don't buy Morgan off the first time." He turned and frowned at Enright. "You know that don't you?"

"Maybe."

"And something else, Forge; Morgan's mother and two brothers still live in the same sod house out there."

"I know that."

"Then why don't we use that against him?"

"In good time," Enright said, "if we have to."

"They might save us a lot of money."

Enright shook his head. "That'll be the last thing we do," he said, "not the first. The surest way I know to make a bear fight is to gang up on its cubs."

Their visit ended like that. With Forge Enright entertaining distaste for Hewton Muller and indifference about Saul Bennett, and with Bennett glaring at the floor, slope-shouldered, hands deep in his pockets and his eyes troubled.

The cowmen were going to get Russ Morgan, not with a hang-rope and guns, but with open hands and money. It galled and burned all the way down with them, too. Wealth and Might, which was Power, was going to knuckle under to an outlaw—a killer and renegade they hadn't been able to do away with in nearly four years.

Bennett found his relief in profanity and angry gestures. Forge Enright rode to Cornell after their visit and got a room at the Cattlemen's Hotel—upstairs over the Cattlemen's Club Saloon—and laid his plans, and because of Enright's plans, Russ found several printed posters nailed to trees in the days which followed. He even found them as far off as Houton Creek, where their presence stirred up considerable interest and aroused grim elation among the squatters. The cowmen were advertising that they wanted to talk to Russ Morgan. The small print said they would meet him anywhere he designated, at any time, and they would come unarmed if he wished it that way.

Russ studied one of the notices, deep in the slough at his camp. The intention behind the offer to meet him was clear enough; they wanted to buy him off. There was a small taste of bitter pleasure to that. He relaxed with his back to an old tree and re-read the paper, then gazed out through the tangle of leaves at the darkened sky, afire with tiny white stars, and smiled to himself. They had had enough—and he hadn't yet begun to fight them, really.

Two days later, over in Houton Creek, a wispy, ageing squatter sidled up to him. " Are you going to meet 'em? " The man asked, with a sly and knowing smile. He regarded the stranger for a long moment before he answered, felt surprised that he was known to a man he was sure he had never seen before.

" What makes you ask that? "

" Everybody's guessing one way or t'other. They look on you as sort of a leader."

It was the same as asking if he was going to take their money. He looked over the man's head at the bustle and dust of Houton Creek's central thoroughfare. At the wagons and sore-shouldered horses, the gaunt men and wan women, the scrawny children. A lemon-yellow sun was frying the entire, sweaty scene, making it ugly to him. He answered without looking down.

" Yes, I'll meet them. I'll listen to them. And they'll offer me a bribe to leave off them."

" What'll you say to that? *That's* what folks want to know, Russ; will you or won't you? "

" No."

The squatter nodded sharply without removing his eyes from the face above his. " Folks'll be glad to hear that, Russ. They'll be gladder to know you mean it, too, because if you'd said no and meant yes, we'd of knowed it."

There was the faintest, mildest undertone of threat to the words. He looked downwards with a stony expression. " If you're so all-fired set on fighting, Mister, why did you wait until I came along to make war-talk? " he asked.

" No," the squatter said softly, " we ain't warriors by

a damned sight, but we *could* be; some of us been so before; only we never had anyone to follow before. I didn't mean to say anything untow'rd, Russ. We're proud o' what you done for us, to a man. At first—folks wasn't sure."

"Are they now?" Russ was thinking of Franklin Minot of Ohio.

"To a man, yessir."

Russ grunted. He had known, if he was successful, a faction would gather to favour him. He also knew that unless such a faction formed, and was strong and loyal, the cowmen would have him killed.

"If you was to raise a finger there'd be fifty men riding with you. Now—tonight, in fact."

The squatter didn't see the brooding glance which watched the ebb and flow of Houton Creek traffic. "There are two sides to everything, Mister," he said. "Maybe as many folks don't believe in what I'm doing as you say, either."

"They do. I know for a fact that they do. That's all folks talk about any more. Russ Morgan an' the way he come back and—"

"Let's see how much of what you've said is wind in the treetops, Mister. Let's see you make this tall talk good. Round up your grangers and fetch them around in back of the liverybarn by tomorrow night. Tell them to bring guns and blankets and whatever else they need—and food. And tell them this: there'll be no end to this once we start it, until the cowmen lay down their guns; until they send their gunmen away and leave the squatters be. If you think they'll fight for that—then get them. I'll be there tomorrow night."

He walked away from the dried-up little squatter without a backward glance. For the first time he was conscious of faces and eyes turning as he passed by.

There was a day and a night to kill. He slept away the night in his hotel room and idled the day away looking after his horse and avoiding people. Thinking, going over and over the plans he had perfected. Now it appeared the second phase of his campaign might be unfolding. Originally, before the fight with Jess Fuller, he had planned things differently. He had wanted to recruit squatters to fight with him at the outset. After the Fuller affair he had altered his intention. Now he saw it as two separate campaigns. The first one, nearly over, was his own individual war. It had been successful enough to stir the countryside and gain him adherents. The second phase, he thought, would be like the first, only intensified. Instead of one man riding himself to a shadow to keep the initiative, now there would be little bands of squatters striking constantly, keeping the cowmen on the defensive, which is exactly the way he had planned it. Offence, he had learned, was the best defence. Knock the cowmen back on their heels. Keep them reeling. If he kept them busy defending their vulnerable empire they would have no time to carry the war to Russ Morgan and the remaining squatters.

He hired a Houton Creek man to take a note he had written to Cornell, and deliver it personally to Forge Enright. He would meet the cowmen; any two they chose to meet with him. The note said that and more; where and how he would meet them.

Then he went to the mercantile and bought a bag of tobacco, stood in the shade of the liverybarn's overhang and smoked impassively, watching the people without appearing to. They knew him, he could see that easily enough.

"Howdy, Russ."

He nodded briefly at the smaller, wiry man standing a few feet in front of him in the roadway's dust. " Howdy; I didn't know I was so easy to recognise," he said.

The young rider laughed dryly. " Well," he said, " tain't no secret who you are, around here no more."

" No? What if I needed a few friends—would folks recognise me then? "

" Sure; I'm one of 'em—plumb to the hilt."

Russ studied the face. There was a rebellious, reckless look to it. " Tell me; have you heard any talk of night-riding squatters gathering anywhere? "

The pale blue eyes twinkled. " I reckon. That's why I'm here. 'Waitin' for Bill Metzen to get back with the rest of 'em."

" Bill Metzen? "

" You know him. Hell—he said he knew you real well. Little old cuss, sort of shrivelled-up looking."

" Oh, sure," Russ said. " What's your name, pardner?"

" Mahoney."

" Mahoney, how would you like to earn twenty dollars right quick? "

" Name it and I'll do it, but I don't want your money."

" Take a pouch to my mother and brothers for me."

" Proud to. When? "

" Right now."

Mahoney's face sobered. Russ understood; anyone seen visiting the Morgan homestead—especially a squatter —was as good as dead. It would be better to wait until dark. Still, the only way to know whether a man could be counted upon was to find out. He waited for the nod and wasn't surprised when Mahoney quirked up a grin and bobbed his head up and down.

" Do you know where Cygnes Swamp is, Mahoney? "

" Sure. I used to hunt 'possums there." The pale

eyes widened. " Is that where you'll be with the others ? "

" Yes."

" Gimme the pouch."

Russ drew it out of his shirt, a heavy little buckskin poke filled with gold and silver coins. Separately, he handed Mahoney a twenty dollar gold piece. The squatter looked wistfully pained. Russ insisted and Mahoney finally took it, blushing furiously and smiling.

" Thanks, Russ. See you at Cygnes Swamp."

He watched his second messenger ride south out of Houton Creek. Now, if he could stay alive a while longer—"

" Hello."

He gazed at her with mixed feelings. In the waning sunlight she was far more handsome than she had been by early dawn. " Don't you belong in Cornell? " he said without pleasantness.

" It's a free country, Mister Morgan. Maybe I should ask if you shouldn't be in hiding; you're an outlaw."

" Only to cowmen, ma'm, and their folks."

" Justice is blind; she could be a cowman or a squatter and still say you were a murderer."

He made a slight gesture with one hand as though to dismiss the topic. Inwardly, he wondered what kept her in Houton Creek when patently her place was in Cornell. " I don't like to argue, ma'm," he said.

Her eyes warmed. " Neither do I, Mister Morgan. Isn't there a common ground we can meet on? "

" I don't know what it could be, Miss Enright."

" I do. You've made the ranchers pay five times over for what they've done in their effort to hold their range. Isn't that—? "

" It isn't *their* range, ma'm, it's free-ground. The ones who own it homestead it. But how much is your father's life worth? Cowmen can't ever pay me for mine."

She looked steadily up at him. " You're going to destroy yourself with those thoughts, Mister Morgan. The Lord knows I understand how you feel—no; I really do—but don't wreck your life harbouring thoughts that won't bring him back."

His colour deepened. " I don't want to talk about it."

" Neither do I." She continued to watch his face, then she sighed. " I suppose you're wondering why I'm over here at all; you probably think I'm spying for my father, don't you? "

" It isn't impossible."

" I've been here a week and haven't even written him. Are you satisfied? "

" It could be dangerous for you—for any cowman."

She made a small, wry smile. " No one's bothered me yet, Mister Morgan."

" Things can change quickly," he said in a dark way. " Did you ever hear the saying that life is the weaving of the wind? "

" No."

" I like it. It means—well—what is to be, will be."

" Maybe," he said, unsure of just what she meant. " Anyway, you'd better go back to your father."

" Not yet, Mister Morgan." She paused. " It's human to take oneself too seriously, isn't it? "

" What do you mean by that? "

" I never did write my father and tell him all those ominous things you asked me to tell him."

" Didn't you think I meant them? "

" I thought you probably meant them that night. I don't think you mean them now, in broad daylight."

" I meant them then, and I mean them now." He fixed his gaze upon her. " I know a saying too, Miss; my dad used to say it every once in a while. ' Let the reason that your course is right and another's course is wrong always be before your mind, son.' "

She was silently regarding his oaken look; the bronzed face and clear eyes; the slightly shaggy hair under its dusty black hat. " You are always right, aren't you? "

He flushed. " No; but I don't like bullies. I don't believe your people have the right to burn and whip and kill people simply because they were on the land first."

" Sir Galahad rides out to fight the dragon, Mister Morgan."

His face flushed darker. In his lifetime ridicule had rarely touched him. He did not know how to cope with it—or her. He said: " I believe what I believe. So do others."

She nodded. " I'm sorry for you, Mister Morgan." Then she walked on by and the dying sunlight seemed to follow in her wake like a soft vermilion shade.

He got his horse from within the barn, saddled it and led it out back where the light lingered. There he hunkered and made another cigarette and smoked it furiously, staring at nothing and feeling the redness of his neck. She was stirring and she was lovely. There was warmth in her expression and understanding in her eyes. Also, there was something mocking about her that gouged him deeply.

He was still hunkered there when the horsemen came. He watched them riding up through the gloom. They were motley, but he had expected as much. Their armament was as varied as their size. One thing he sought in each face, and found: a grimness, a set to the jaw and a hardness to the eye. Without a word of greeting he mounted and beckoned to them to follow. Bill Metzen took the lead, fell in behind Russ and threw out his chest.

CHAPTER 3

" Fight—That's It In One Word! "

He led them to his camp in the slough and there he showed Bill Metzen how to make a roster of names and detail men for round-the-clock sentry duty. When he spoke in his curt, confident way, the squatters recognised the sound of authority. When he called them all together that first night and stood like a shaggy bear before them, speaking in his deep-booming way, they acknowledged him as a leader.

" Fight—that's it in one word. Fight for your rights and your lives. Ask nothing—give nothing. The cowmen've had their way, now we'll have our's. When I send you word, you'll act on it without delay. But do nothing without an order." He counted them as he spoke; thirty-seven. There were older men with bushy beards and stony faces; younger men like Mahoney, restless with rebelliousness, and with hatred like a banner in their faces. He liked what he saw and told them so.

When he finished speaking, a gaunt, bearded man, like a scarecrow in his patched clothing and shapeless hat, arose. He clutched a musket of ancient origin with a beautifully inlaid maple stock; a Pennsylvania rifle, which had once been the tool of all early riflemen.

" My name's Lavender. Burt Lavender." The old voice threw out an echo that lingered in the dark places of the swamp. " I'm not ag'n killing, Mister Morgan, not by a long sight, especially when it's cowmen do the dyin', but if there was a crafty way to do this I got it in my head it'd be a sight better done that way. I don't like seein' my friends and neighbours shot down."

Russ spoke coldly. " If a thing's worth fighting for, Mister Lavender, then it's worth dying for. But if some of you have cooled off since we got down here, I'll do nothing to keep you in the camp. You can go whenever you've a mind to."

He walked away from them after that. Behind was a silence, a motionless silence while they watched his shadow dwindle and lose itself among the tangled trees and deadfalls.

The squatters lounged around their little fires and they had lots of thoughts, but mainly they accepted him as their leader and none spoke against him. He was a legend—had been one before they ever put eyes on him—and if, up close, he became like black iron, why then that was his way. Regardless, he was their leader and think as they might of other things, they knew very well they could not find another like him. They approved his spirit of resistance, his wolf-wiliness, and while men like Burt Lavender had doubts that he was *of* them, none doubted but that he was *for* them. Right then that alone mattered, for each of them knew the day of battle was approaching.

When Mahoney rode into the slough past the cordon of sentries, he was as surprised at their numbers as Russ himself had been. He put up his horse and went among the little groups visiting until he found Bill Metzen, with whom he had been close for several years. He dropped down at Metzen's fire and grinned. " Now we're *doin'* something, Bill," he said. " Now we got strength, and hell's fire's going to bust loose." He made a cigarette and smoked it, firelight shining over his sweat-shiny face in an oily way.

" Now there'll be the devil to pay."

" I had it pictured different," Metzen said. " It sort of

scares a feller."

Mahoney looked up quickly. "How? You knew there'd be fighting, Bill. What else can there be? We got the man we need to lead us; the cowmen'll cinch up, too. There'll be fighting and by God, I'm all for it."

"I can't put it into words exactly. I just got this feeling about how things're going to turn out. Morgan's different from what I thought he'd be."

Mahoney's pale eyes burned out from beneath his hatbrim. "It don't mean he's not the best leader just because you don't understand him, Bill. Maybe I won't understand him either. I reckon I don't even expect to. All I ask is that he lead us in a body against the cowmen; that's all I ask and I know damned well he figures to it. I also know when the smoke clears away we'll be top-dog, Bill. Cowmen'll leave us alone after that, too, you watch."

Metzen turned his head as though the effort was a thing he was fighting against. Looking into Mahoney's face he saw zeal there, and was fascinated by it. He turned away with a stirring in his own spirit.

"He's a strange cuss, Mahoney," he said, "and besides that I got a strange feeling about how this is all going to end."

"You're entitled to your feeling, Bill," Mahoney said. "All of us are. All I say is that we never had leadership before and now we got it. Look at what he done singlehanded. He raided and robbed them and not a cowman so much as got a shot at him up to now. With us," Mahoney made a savage smile and gestured with one arm, "he'll give them the lickin' of their lives—and they've got it coming. No matter what we do to them they got it coming, Bill. Am I right?"

"Yes, you're right," and Metzen shrugged to indicate

the conversation was closed so far as he was concerned, but in the background of his eyes the premonition lingered as strong, as dark and forbidding as ever.

Metzen went down on one elbow and gazed around among the other campfires. Men were there in relaxed solemnity. Some were smoking, some whittling, a few talking or eating, while here and there a man lay full length upon the grass with his arms under his head, looking up through the moon-dappled splendour that came in a pale pattern through tree limbs. It was a comfortable, orderly encampment.

When Metzen regarded Mahoney again it was with the inner knowledge of how simply and directly Mahoney's mind worked. But his own mind didn't work that way; the troubled feeling within was solid. He lay back and sighed, his expression philosophical; in every band of men there was at least one worrier; he was that one in Cygnes Swamp.

Mahoney arose, the music of his spurs breaking into the drone of silence. He walked over where Russ sat, back against a hairy boulder.

"I'm back," he said, and dropped down. When Russ gazed at him without speaking, he said: "I delivered it and they all look fine. They asked a heap of questions. I didn't know how much you wanted told so I just said you were well and hearty."

"Thanks," Russ said. There was no curve of moon-light to give him a sense of time, no sun that grew to a height then dropped off to indicate a passage of hours. Just the scudding, frayed mists of night hours with minutes trooping towards an end, and the dead grey of the mist, diluted and blanched-looking.

"Mahoney; do you know a feller named Lavender?"

Mahoney nodded carelessly. "Yeah, I know him.

Old time trapper and hunter. Is he here, too?"

"He's here. It sticks in my head that we might have someone here who might be a little for the cowmen."

Mahoney looked up quickly. "Lavender? Naw, not him. Why, he had a few old cows on Skull Creek two years ago and the cowmen run them off because the old man was free-grazing them. He's been down on cowmen ever since."

"Maybe not him, then," Russ said. "Do you know Metzen very well?"

"I've known Bill a long time. I'll tell you about him. He's religious and sort of on the gloomy side; it's his nature to be that way, but he's a good man. He wouldn't sell you out. He might get mad and read you off, but he wouldn't sell you out."

"A lot of squatters are religious people," Russ said. "How about you?"

Mahoney grinned crookedly. "I believe in sweat and rain and black earth. That's about all."

Russ smiled. "Me too," he said, and closed one door of the conversation. "Now, look here." He smoothed off a patch of ground with one hand. "I'm going to meet the cowmen tomorrow," drawing a diagram as he spoke, holding Mahoney's attention, Russ traced his plan in the moonlit dust. "Here—where this pebble is—there will be a stake. That's about six hundred feet west of this gully. Now, I want you to take the squatters down into that arroyo and keep them there, out of sight. I don't trust the cowmen. They may bring a gun-crew with them. If they do, and I holler, you fellers shoot, but remember one thing, keep hidden because if any of you are recognised there will be more burnt out soddies and gun-shot livestock—and maybe widows. You understand what I want?"

"I understand."

They talked a while longer then each retired for what was left of the night. The bivouac settled into silence. Phantoms moving without sound were the guards changing. Out where the horses were, two men cradling carbines talked in low tones and sat hunkered under loosely-held blankets. The night wore on . . .

The meeting hour drew closer as the morning sun climbed, and in the squatter camp bustling activity culminated when the body of men rode out, behind Bill Metzen and Mahoney, heading for the arroyo. They were well into its twisting, crumbly depths before two slow-riding horsemen appeared over the edge of prairie far out, heading for a stake driven into the ground with a red rag around it, like a miniature turban.

There was no movement in the emptiness, but neither Bennett nor Forge Enright were deluded. They knew about the arroyo; knew also that it probably held a friend or two of Morgan's; maybe a dozen friends. They rode up to the stake, dismounted and squatted down in glum silence. Bennett began worrying up a cigarette, blue eyes darting over the lip of paper from time to time.

Russ watched them from the dry-wash; let them hunker out there until Bill Metzen came in from the south and reported that no riders had followed Enright and Bennett any farther north than the Minot place. Then Mahoney came up with the news that no one had gotten between them and the slough, so it appeared that the cowmen were in earnest. He mounted and rode up out of the arroyo, urged his horse towards the motionless, hunched over men squatting in what shade their horses made.

They watched him approach and neither moved. It was as though they were made of stone. They had expected a large man, but the two-gun man coming towards them was big enough to blot out the sun when he hauled up in front of them, studied both a moment, then swung down.

Enright's ice-chip eyes never flickered; their veil of inwardness was more dense than usual. Saul Bennett stood up first, feeling dwarfed and uncomfortable.

" I'm Saul Bennett of SB," he said.

" Forge Enright of the Texas Company."

Russ hooked his thumbs in his shell-belt without nodding. " All right," he said. " Here I am."

Enright fished in his pocket for his pipe and pouch, filled the pipe and lit it. When he had a good head of smoke up, he said, " We want to do a little trading, Morgan. This business has gone far enough."

" Do *you* think it has? " Russ said, and Bennett's eyes flashed out at him. Forge Enright lowered his head as though occupied with his pipe. He spoke a moment later.

" Morgan, we'll give you ten thousand dollars to ride off and never come back."

Russ shook his head without speaking. Bennett jammed his hands into his trouser pockets. His face was ruddy and swollen looking but he refrained from speaking.

Enright's anger flared briefly. It showed in his brittle, wide stare. Russ met it head-on.

" Listen, Morgan; sooner or later you're going to get it, if you keep this up. You'd be 'way ahead to take the money."

" By my tally," Russ replied, " you owe the squatters about five times that much, Enright."

" Man," Bennett said thickly, " you're talking crazy. Listen; we'll give you twenty thousand in cash to leave the country and never come back. Twenty thousand,

Morgan." He watched Russ with lizard-like intensity, standing stiffly erect with sweat from the smashing sun running under his shirt.

"You could offer me five times that much and I wouldn't take it."

"You're making a bad mistake," Enright said quietly. "You've made money off us—off the cowmen—but don't think things are going to stay that way because they aren't. We can out-fight you, and match you two to one in dollars, Morgan. Use your head; if you keep this up there'll be a range war sure as God made green apples. Squatters don't win range wars—they never have and it won't start to happen here. Take the twenty thousand and slope."

Russ let a moment of silence hang between them before he replied, then he said: "It might happen here; I think it will and I'll tell you why. You fellers've made the grangers hate the sight of a cowman. I draw my strength from that and one other thing. The biggest mistake you could've made—and did make—was to ask me to meet with you. That cost you a lot in the eyes of squatters and your own people."

"It was to save your squatters that we even considered coming out here," Bennett said.

"Oh hell," Russ said in scorn, "that's pure wind and we all know it. The reason you fellers came was because I've cost you a lot of money, to start with, and to finish with, because you're afraid I'll organise the squatters—who out-number you about three-to-one—and if I do that, you know cussed well no matter how many men you hire, you'll lose." Russ let out a big gush of breath. "And I'll tell you something else; I haven't begun to fight you yet."

Stung, Enright said, "We haven't begun to fight yet either, Morgan. We haven't begun to drive out the squatters—not like we intend to do if you turn down this offer of twenty thousand dollars. And don't overlook something else, either; if we hound them bad enough, a lot of them'll hate *you* even more than they hate us. We'll make it plenty plain that it's *you* we want to get rid of—not them."

" They won't believe that; not after what you've been doing to them for all these years."

" Some will," Bennett said. " And when we put up the reward for you a little, some of those who *do* believe it will try to collect the money on your carcass. Morgan; you'll have enemies in front of you and behind you. I'm betting it'll be one of your own people who'll finally kill you—from behind."

Anger showed on all their faces. It was Forge Enright who endeavoured to inject calmness back into the conversation. He said: " Morgan; we can hire a man-killer for a thousand dollars. Imagine how many will ride to Cornell from all over the West, for ten thousand dollars. But that's beside the point; what we want is peace. Be reasonable, man; take the twenty thousand. Use it any way you want only stay out of this country. What can you do by staying and fighting? You'll get a lot of people killed. We're strong, Morgan; we've got right on our side."

" What right have you got? "

" We were here first. We took this land from Indians. We made our own law here. We've tamed the country and made it pay us a living."

Russ snorted. " What kind of talk is that? " he asked. " Hell's fire, Enright, you weren't here first, the Indians were. You took the land from them. Now you're going to lose it to farmers and you're doing exactly what the Indians did—you're trying to hold it with no more right

—with *less* right, actually. Listen; if you fellers hadn't been so short-sighted you'd have bought this country; got title to it, but you didn't think you'd ever have to. You have guns; they set you up here and you figured they'd keep you here. Well, they won't. Not now; not with emigrants coming in droves. You had your chance to own it and you didn't think it good enough to buy, but now, when decent, law-abiding folks come in, you scare them off, beat them out, shoot them down. You're worse than the Indians were, in my sight."

Enright's pipe was out, his mouth locked harshly around it. " All right," he said. " Think of what Saul said. A ten thousand dollar reward for you, dead, will make it only a matter of time. What good are you to those people dead?"

"You may be right," Russ said. "You may get me killed—maybe even by a squatter, like you say—but before I'd dead I give you my word your outfits'll lose five times what it'll cost you to down me. One man's life isn't important, maybe, nor five or ten men's lives, but what those squatters stand for *is* important. You had my father murdered. He wasn't important—but what happened because you killed him *is* important. Because of him I'm standing here now. Because of him, you have lost a lot of money and livestock. You didn't think it might be like that when you had him killed, did you?"

Russ fixed Forge Enright with a flat stare. Both of them ignored Saul Bennett, who was staring intently at a wisp of movement over at the edge of the gully. Bennett's heavy, normally ruddy face was pale.

Enright moved abruptly to catch the reins to his horse. Without a word he mounted. When Bennett remained rooted, he said, " Come on, Saul; we're wasting time here." Then the cold pale eyes moved to Russ's face.

"Do you believe that stuff, Morgan?"

"So would you if you were in my place."

"No I wouldn't."

Russ shrugged and Bennett grunted into the saddle. His horse fidgetted, wrung its tail several times as he settled deeper upon its back, still watching the lip of the gully.

"Take the twenty thousand, Morgan. That's my advice to you."

"Thanks. The last thing I want is advice from a cowman."

Enright knocked out his pipe and pocketed it. "Morgan," he said detachedly, "I knew a man like you once. He was an Indian. His own people killed him. I don't think there's anything for men like you except that kind of a fate."

"There can be worse things than dying, Enright."

"All right, Morgan, we'll fight. Now listen to me. You want peace for your damned settlers. It'll never be as long as there's a cowman, and that's a fact. Not just out here but everywhere in the West. Free-range and squatters just plain can't go together. It'll be cowman or squatter; one will go under or the other will, and today you've called the shot for this part of the country. Remember that, Morgan." Enright lifted his reins. "You can't win."

Bennett reined out when Enright wheeled and began to ride away. Russ watched them go. Once, several hundred yards down the land, Bennett twisted his neck and peered back, then swiped at the sweat on his face and said, "Forge; he's crazy as a coot. By God, he's asking to be killed."

Forge Enright rode along in thoughtful silence for a

mile, then he said: "Crazy? Bennett, once I saw a Cheyenne buck go to his medicine man and get annointed with magic salve against soldier-bullets, then he charged a company of cavalry and they all fired at him. *I saw this, Bennett.* When he was finally killed, we went over and looked at him. There wasn't a bullet hole in him anywhere."

"Well; how'd they kill him?"

"A soldier cut him down with his sabre."

"How's that fit in with Morgan?"

"I don't know, except that Morgan's got the same kind of outlook. He's got it in his head, some way, that he's got a purpose in life. That's the hardest kind of man to kill."

"Ten thousand dollars'll hire a heap of killing, Forge."

By the time Enright and Bennett were specks in the distance, Russ had repeated his conversation with them to the squatters. It was hot down in the arroyo, but a lot of the perspiration came from excitement, too. When the meeting was no longer news, Russ led them back towards the slough. As they were entering the woods, he raised his arm to halt them.

"Now let's move our camp, boys," he said. "From now on I don't think we'll want to stay long in one place. Maybe we won't get much rest, either."

Later, when the shadows were lengthening, he led them to the headwaters of a creek which coursed crookedly down from the high ridges of the distant foothills and lost itself upon the prairie. From that eminence they could see for miles; no cowmen could surprise them. Up there, Russ spent days organising the men into small, hard-riding parties. He taught them how to fade into shadows and out-ride the devil. He drilled them in shooting, in living off the land, in leaving false tracks. Even Bill Metzen, whose misgivings had loomed so large for a while, was caught up in the general enthusiasm. None of the preachments Russ taught were ignored. Every footnote from the book of outlawry, Russ knew so well, was absorbed by Bill and the others, until their leader was satisfied. When he finally led them down from the heights they exulted with an *esprit de corps* none would have dreamed of ten days before. Morgan's Men they called themselves, and under that designation were destined to write their saga into the annals of the West.

He led them towards a holding ground where scouts had kept him informed that SB was marshalling a big herd of topped-out critters for a drive. They went like wraiths in the darkness until the soft-distant lowing of cattle was clear, and the pungent odour of a great herd filled their lungs.

"Mahoney; take half the men and come in from the west. They won't smell you because the wind's from the east. If you're quiet enough they won't hear you until you're on them. Metzen; take a couple of men and ride for the soddies. Tell the people when they see a big bonfire tomorrow night to ride for it."

"They'll want to know why, Russ."

"Tell them; say because we're raiding the cowmen tonight and they'll strike back sure, so all the squatters've got to stand together from now on, or pull out."

Metzen moved among the bunched up, motionless horsemen. Mahoney reined closer to Russ. "Now?" he asked.

"Just a minute. I'll need five men. You take your bunch and hit the herd. Keep it moving. Drive for the hills. You'll lose some, but don't go back for a single head. Keep the men together and don't stop for anything. I'll set up an ambush between you and the SB crew. We'll hold them as long as we can, then we'll stay behind you, covering the flank. All set?"

"All set," Mahoney said.

Russ turned to the listening men. "Riddle, McCann, Martin, Balester, Wiley—stay with me. The rest of you go with Mahoney. Now remember; let the cut-backs go and don't let the SB separate you." He tightened his hold on the reins. "Let's go!"

Through the clear night air the SB nighthawks heard their hoofbeats. They sat rigid and wondering, began to call out to one another, and when they were satisfied it was strangers they raced towards the main camp yelling and brandishing their pistols—but not firing for fear of starting a stampede.

At the SB camp, riders tumbled out of soogans and pawed for their boots, hats, and guns. The beating, insistent drumroll of hoofbeats came closer and sharper. The riders raced for their horses, saddled up amid the howls of their companions and the rising dirge of noise among the aroused, nervous cattle.

Mahoney, at the head of the flying wedge, struck the herd with a shout that rang out over the other sounds and in the SB camp a man swore mightily and yelled out: "Squatters!"

The cattle gave out a panicky bellow of fear. From the west came orange flashes of gunfire and the earth shook under the hooves of hundreds of terrified, stampeding animals. The earth became a sea of shaggy backs and pale horns that clicked and rattled like a thousand rattlesnakes. Little red eyes glowed with unreasoning panic. The stampede was in full swing, a spreading juggernaut of flesh and blood, a fear-tossed tidal wave nothing could stop.

Bennett's riders hastened westward, following the gun flashes and the faint echoes of throaty yells. They hauled up in a long, wild slide when more squatters appeared out of the night in front of them. Guns exploded and men cried out. The SB riders broke in all directions, whirled towards their camp and rallied upon a howling, wild-eyed foreman, who had lost his hat, but not his ability to blaspheme. The foreman led them back towards the hidden attackers. A ripple of gunfire slowed them. It wasn't until the wrathful foreman's horse went down in a hurtling sprawl, sending the rider through the air like a pinwheel, that the other SB men drew up, the fight gone out of them.

Satisfied, Russ led his raiders in pursuit of Mahoney and the SB herd. It was hours later before he found the men, but along the way he passed little groups of bewildered cattle, tongues out and panting. Mahoney loomed up finally, a loose-jointed silhouette on a lean and sinewy bay horse, riding easily in the wake of the cattle. There was a black pistol riding lightly in one hand and the cords of his neck were stark-etched in the gloom. Russ had to shout to make himself heard.

"Slow up; save your horse. The cattle are headed right. Nothing'll stop them until they give out." Mahoney slowed, holstered his gun and looked over his shoulder. "They aren't coming," Russ said. "We stopped them back at the holding ground."

Mahoney wiped his forehead with his sleeve and smiled. "Guess we'd better see where the others are," he said.

"Wait a minute. Listen; when the critters've run themselves down, let them rest a spell then drive them into the hills. Take your time. Put a couple of men to watching your back-trail. If SB follows don't fight unless you have to. What we want is to push this herd a long day's drive into the mountains; get it too footsore to come back for a while."

"You mean keep it moving all day tomorrow, too?"

"Yes. Drop it when you've done your work, then bring your men back to the prairie, but don't cross the open country until after dark. You'll see the bonfire; head for that."

"I understand."

"One thing to remember, Mahoney; you've got to make your best time tonight. They can't track you in the dark. After sunup they can spot you by the dust-cloud."

"We'll be damned hard to find once we get into the brush country. See you tomorrow night, Russ."

The herd drew ahead, its shadowy riders moving slower now, more phantom-like than ever, as Russ swung northward in a tight lope. Inwardly, he felt exultant and his thoughts soared. Twenty thousand dollars, Bennett? There was half that much in the herd it had required one night to acquire. When he could no longer hear the trumpeting bellow of wet-cows separated from their calves, he slowed to a fast walk and rode steadily northward for several hours until his attention was snagged by a faint-distant fingering of red light. A shaft of fire licking straight up in the small hours. He squinted his eyes and stared.

"There were other night-riders out tonight, too," he said to his horse, and struck a course directly towards the light.

The closer he got, the more panic grew in him. A dark yawning well of fear and knowledge. When he was close enough to smell the fire his throat and eyes were dry.

He knew whose soddy that was, with the flame backgrounding it. He could see the scrawny little orchard and the silhouette of men and horses limned against the crackling haystack, which was the symbol of the cowmen's fury.

He had purposefully avoided going near this one soddy because he wanted them to dis-associate it from him. Now he knew that had been a senseless thing to imagine would happen. Recalling Forge Enright's impassive, rock-hard features, his deep-set, calculating and thoughtful eyes, he knew that his greatest mistake had been to think the cowmen would suffer his mother and brothers to stay in the land unmolested.

A dozen recriminations crowded his mind. He should have detailed men to guard the place. He should have gone home first; got his family to leave the country.

The flames were pale as though at the height of their intensity, which meant the fire hadn't been started until late in the night. Probably about the time he was riding towards the SB herd. Maybe the two parties had even passed close to one another on their separate missions of vengeance.

There was no caution left in him when he drew up and threw himself from the saddle. He counted the men outlined against the flames while scarcely heeding them. They weren't cowmen, he saw that in one glance. Only one was facing him, face shiny with sweat, mouth twisted: Bill Metzen.

He pushed past them without speaking and stopped where a twisting circle of light drenched the churned earth in front of the soddy. His tongue was like wood, locked behind his teeth.

CHAPTER 4

The Blood Remembers!

Metzen and the others were rigid, their faces contorted, made evil and strange by the firelight. A smell of burnt flesh was strong in the night air. When Russ pushed through and halted, he caught the scent before he saw the unmoving body at his feet. Across the naked shoulders was burnt with a terrible purpose, two words: Just Begun.

Understanding and a swell of fury swept over him.

Bill knelt and turned the boy over. The red-glowing hay fire touched the unconscious features. Russ dropped down with one palm upon the warm, packed earth. Metzen put an ear to the boy's mouth. There was no faint sigh against his flesh. He looked up.

"Who's got a piece of glass or metal?"

Someone had and held it out. Metzen bent again, his eyes squinted towards the shiny surface—and it came; the vague misting over from expelled breath.

"He's alive, Russ."

The others edged around to shield the battered body from the heat until Russ picked up his brother, cradled him in his big arms like a baby and made for the broken door of the soddy, a place he hadn't entered in almost five years, stooping low to duck under the dazed header.

He put Will upon his bunk and salved his back where the branding iron had left its message, and sent the others to seek his mother and other brother. There was no trace of his mother, but the men found Jim—he of the hot pride and quick temper. They found him in a dark corner of the gutted soddy with an old single-shot Army carbine lying across his legs. He was dead; shot in the chest four times and once through the head—up close—so that the powder-burn made a third eye.

Russ helped dig the grave and bury Jim. He said nothing, and when they rode away he carried Will in his arms, nor did he seem to tire although the trail was long. Back at the camp he remained silent. He stayed beside the branded boy through a painful period of delirium, salving the swollen flesh and bathing the red, working face.

It was there he discovered that he possessed the same strange gentleness his father had possessed, for under his hands young Will's flesh became soothed and cool, except where the words were scored deeper, and his brother regained his wits under the expert care. As soon as Will opened his eyes, Russ detailed him to the care of others, for it was getting late in the day, and rode down to supervise the gathering of wood for the bonfire. In his mind was an icy need to kill.

When the last rays of the sun paled he lit the bonfire himself, and stood there with the others, tired and dirty, watching the growing conflagration vying with the dwindling twilight.

He waited. They all waited. They waited a long time, until well after nightfall, before the squatters began to appear, riding stealthily with fear plain in their faces, clutching whatever armament they possessed, which in some cases was nothing more than stout clubs.

He watched some circle widely around the fire, sniffing for a cowman trap. Others, in defensive groups, rode straight into the light and peered around them until, seeing men they knew, they got down and stood awkwardly at ease. Quite a number of the mounted men had bundles behind their cantles. Those, Russ knew, intended to stay.

Bill Metzen, squatting with a carbine balanced across his legs, grey-faced and whisker-stubbled, counted the newcomers. When he finally arose and faced Russ, he said, " By my count there are sixty of them, Russ. One thing sticks in my mind though; there may be some spies among them."

" It won't matter, Bill. After what's happened tonight it won't be any secret what we mean to do."

" If you tell them too much, though, we could ride into an ambush, Russ."

" I won't tell them anything of our plans, Bill. That's not why I asked them here anyway." He suggested that Metzen move among them, see if he could recognise any among them who might not be a squatter, then he raised his arm for silence and the waiting men grew still.

" Listen, boys," he said loudly, " you hated me five years ago because you thought I'd brought trouble to you. By now you know damned well it would have come anyway. And after I came back this time there were some of you thought the same thing again—that Morgan meant more trouble for you. Now you ought to know a sight better. As long as any squatters are here the cowmen'll go on riding and whipping, burning and killing. They mean to keep this cow-country, and with me or without me, you're going to get shot and whipped and burnt out.

" Some of us have been taking their war right back to them. We mean to go right on fighting them until a man can plough his field without being assassinated. We believe being right counts for something and we aim to fight for our rights. You have more right here than the cowmen have; you have patents to your land. All the cowmen have is guns."

" That's enough," someone called out harshly.

"No it isn't, boys; guns aren't enough by a damned sight. First you got to have *right*; all right; we've *got* right. Now what we need is guns to match their guns. That'll break the balance. Now—the reason we wanted you to come here tonight was to find out who among you will ride with us. The cowmen want a range war and by God it's our intention to see they get all the fighting they want—for all time! We're going to carry their war into their own land for a change; into their homes and camps, wherever we can find them. We're going to give them a taste of being burnt out and whipped off and shot down. We're going to roll into them and never stop until they've had enough. To do that we need more men—more guns —which of you'll join us?"

When the squatters began to stamp and shout, Bill Metzen raised up on his toes beside Russ and said, "Send back the boys and family men, Russ."

But it wasn't possible to make himself heard for a while so he couldn't tell them he didn't want youngsters or men with children until the tumult dwindled a little. Even while he was talking the mumbling droned on.

"And remember, boys," he thundered, "there'll be some of you who won't ride back."

That stilled the harsh grumble of voices and made way for a sobering fear to come among them. At last they were silent. Metzen held up a paper, waved it back and forth.

"Those of you who're ready to join right now, come up here and put your names down," he said. "Those of you who'll be staying at home remember—we need spies to fetch us news and we might need messengers; places to hide the wounded; you can do those things for us."

"Hey, Morgan," a stalwart man called out, "we heard a rumour this evenin' they hit your place. Is that true?"

"Yes," Russ said, "it's true. They killed one of my brothers and took my mother hostage. My other brother is in our camp. They branded two words on his back—Just Begun."

"What's that mean?"

"It means they've just begun to fight us, and I'll tell you this; a man capable of running a brand on a boy's bare back is capable of any crime under the sun—so don't forget that, because from now on the fighting's going to be bitter and bloody. If we don't stand together we'll be shot separately."

The mob broke up into little groups. Over the sounds of their voices the bonfire crackled. Russ and Bill Metzen stood together watching. The grangers were persecuted men—hard men who had followed a star which was now dyed red—neither boys to be easily stirred, nor heroes seeking an outlet for bravery, but just men with a heartbreaking disillusionment in them, deep-groovings of pain and suffering. They were men who understood what a chance was, once taken, so they discussed it beforehand. It was, of course, essential that they band together in defence; all knew that; it was the matter of *offence* they talked of now.

Finally, when the fire was dying down, a burly man in much-mended clothing strode to the forefront of the crowd. "I'm Jason Corning," he said in a voice as rough as the south side of a rock. "I'm a late-comer out here, but I been fightin' since I was this high—and by God I'll fight again. We'll all be outlaws either way, as I see it, so I'm ready, Morgan. Where do I sign up for Morgan's Men?"

Out of the crowd came nineteen who were grim and fierce and capable looking. Russ appraised each one as they formed into a slatternley line in front of Bill Metzen.

Of the sixty-odd who had come, six demurred; they were leaving the country, wanted no part of a range war. The rest were family men and many volunteered to ride, but Russ said no, maybe later they might be needed, but right now they weren't. From them he selected men whose conversations proved they were wiser than appearance made them. These he designated spies and while Metzen was copying down names, Russ told them what information he wanted, and how they could contact him.

Shortly after Metzen was finished, the meeting broke up. Russ rode to the uplands encampment with the newcomers and met a bone-weary Mahoney en route.

"Get chased?" he asked.

"No, they never even got close, but my rear's tender enough to feel a shadow ten miles off, from all that ridin'." Mahoney swung in beside Russ. "How'd the meeting go?"

Russ rocked his head backwards. "Those are the recruits; about twenty, I think. Did the SB try to catch up?"

"Somebody sure did, I don't know whether it was SB or not. A big posse of them. We had too big a start though; they didn't come much farther than the first brushy ridge. By the way, we drifted a few of the fattest critters over near the camp and left them there in case you favour a little fresh beef."

"Good idea," Russ said, and branched off from the others when in sight of the camp. He went where Will lay with a shirt over his purpling back, sat down and accepted a tin dish of stew from the older man who had stayed with his brother. The younger Morgan's colour was good. There was pain in his eyes but they were clear.

"Want to tell me about it, Will?"

"They struck like rattlers, Russ. We hardly saw them before the shooting started."

"Mother?"

"First," Will Morgan said, "when they came up she told us not to pick up our guns—not to fight them. She said they'd only kick in the doors looking for you, that they weren't after us. But Jim and me—we knew it wouldn't be like that as soon as we could hear them calling to one another. By then I think she knew it wasn't going to be like that too, but she still said for us not to fight them. Jim fetched his gun and when they came storming up he fired through a wall-notch and got one of them."

"I know how Jim died," Russ said. "We buried him."

"After they got inside they grabbed maw—five of them —and held her. Made her watch while they branded me. After that—I don't know what happened."

"Before that, Will; did you recognise any of them?"

"I couldn't. It was dark; Jim put the candles out when the fight started.."

"What did they say about maw?"

"One man said she was pretty hefty to carry. They swore at her when she hung back begging them not to brand me."

"That was all?"

"About all I can remember, Russ. They didn't hit her, if that's what you want to know. They cussed considerable but I'm sure they didn't hit her—at least while I was conscious. Russ? When they got inside, Jim was in the corner; what did they—?"

"Have you had supper?"

"Yes."

"Get some sleep, Will, we'll talk about that later." He went down where the others were cooking supper. There was a hush when he approached. The recruits looked up with understanding; they had been told. Bill Metzen held up a steaming cup of coffee. Russ squatted down when he accepted it.

"How is he?" Metzen said.

"A lot better, Bill."

Metzen poked at the coals with a sharpened stick. "And your mother," he said. "A hostage?"

"It'd have to be that. I reckon they meant to take the whole family, but when Jim started shooting—"

"Yeah. They probably meant to capture all three of them, brand 'em one at a time and turn 'em loose to make you quit."

Russ swished the dregs in the cup, cast them out and put the cup down. "They might have had that in mind. One thing—if they'd taken all three as hostages they'd have had a real whip hand, Bill." He walked over where his bedroll was and kicked off his boots, lay back listening to the camp grow quiet as time passed, and finally he slept

The dawn came hours later, cool and grey. A pure mist floated among the treetops and washed the stain of night away. From the underbrush came the drowsy calls of birds and the grating, scolding sounds of rodents. When he sat up to pull on his boots men were arising, twisting and stretching, calling out softly to one another. Several sentries with blankets over their shoulders edged up to a new fire and poured tepid coffee for themselves. Bill Metzen came up and squatted down with a tight look around his mouth.

"We didn't see all of it last night, Russ," he said. "Two more fellers rode in to join us this morning."

"Go on."

"They killed Norman Tidd and Murray Ashcraft last night."

"Attacked their places?"

Metzen nodded. "Caught them as they were saddling up to ride to the bonfire."

Russ said nothing. His face tightened, the eyes darkening.

"They must have known about the meeting. The fellers who just came in said they saw them. There was a lot of them and they were hitting every homestead they came across as though they knew there would be only women and kids there; as though they wouldn't run into any resistance."

"Tidd and Ashcraft resisted though."

"And got killed," Metzen said.

Russ ran crooked fingers through his hair. The fires of anger were banked against cold dread. He knew what the cowmen would do to their hostage the next time Morgan's Men struck. The knowledge made his spirit darken with a depth of fear.

Metzen straightened up and leaned against a tree without speaking.

"As soon as the men have eaten have them mount up, Bill."

Metzen walked away, down towards the smoking fires, and Russ went over where Will lay. To the old man who was nursing the boy he said: "Keep him here; use plenty of salve and feed him up."

"You ridin'?" the old man asked. Russ nodded and watched his brother awaken, stifle a groan as he worked his way up on one elbow, tousel-headed and puffy-eyed.

" Russ? Are you riding? "

" Yes; you take it easy. Your friend'll take care of you. I'll be back as soon as I can."

" Wish I could go with you."

" You aren't able to be up and about yet, Will. Maybe next time."

He left Will, went to the creek, washed in the icy water and listened to the activity behind him. Men were talking, rattling horse equipment, joking about the amount of ammunition they intended to use the next time they met the cowmen, and over it all was the fragrance of the little cooking fires. By the time Russ was ready, the squatters were saddled up and waiting. On full stomachs they were in good moods with much joking and hazing going back and forth. The undercurrent was unanimously in favour of seeking out the cowmen and fighting them. Mahoney's voice arose over the rest briefly.

" They'll fight. Give a cowman a target and he'll shoot at it. They'll fight all right, make no mistake about that."

Bill Metzen was close to Russ. With an ironic grin he said, " 'Ever see a greener crew of Crusaders? "

Before Russ answered, Mahoney sniffed. " Crew of what? "

" Crusaders, you ignorant dog thief."

A ripple of mild laughter arose. Mahoney fixed Metzen with a squinted stare. " Listen, you holy joe ... Well; that better not mean what it sounds like it could mean."

" Crusaders, you fugitive from a razor, are men who fight for something they believe in."

" Oh, Mahoney said. " Well; folks don't fight unless they *do* believe."

" No? " Metzen answered quickly. " How about hired gunmen? "

Mahoney squirmed. "It's too early for me to argue good," he said, and swung into the saddle.

When Russ mounted the others did likewise. Guns bristled among them. Russ swung to face them. "Listen to me," he said, knowing they would follow without knowing where he would lead them but wishing to explain what he had in mind, regardless. "Listen and remember, boys. Last night the cowmen killed Tidd and Ashcraft. You've heard that by now. You know what they did to my family. Those words they burnt into my brother's back aren't a bluff. From now it's going to be a fight to the hilt for all of us on both sides. Today we're going to hit them where it'll hurt the most."

"In broad daylight?" Lavender called out, aghast.

"Yes, in broad daylight. We're not coyotes like they are. We don't have to sneak around in the night, so we're going to hit 'em by daylight and dark, both. From now, we don't stop attacking, either. We've all waited a long time for this, but you want to remember a couple of things. They'll give you no quarter. If they catch any of you—you'll hang from the nearest tree.

"Now—we could hit their cow camps and ranches, but they'd still have their rallying point at Cornell. If they lost their town they'd be as scattered as their ranches are scattered—all over a hundred miles of country."

"Attack Cornell?" a thin, grey-haired rider said incredulously.

"Yes; that's where we're going now. If some of you want to drop out, now's the time to do it." He turned to Metzen. "Bill; when we get within sight of Cornell, take whatever men you need and tear down the telegraph line. Make it a good, clean break."

Metzen nodded.

"The rest of you—we'll divide up as we ride. Some

of you under Mahoney will ride out around the town and seal it off to the south. When they see us coming in force some'll try to get away. Since we'll be riding from the north they'll head south. Mahoney? You understand what I want?"

"Sure do. I'll take care of it."

"The rest of you will be split into two parties. Half will ride into Cornell with me. The rest will scatter out on the prairie around Cornell at spaced intervals and intercept any riders who try to sneak out." He leaned over his saddlehorn looking at them. "Don't be soft with them, boys. If you are they'll get the drop on you. Disarm every person you see. Take what you need to set up your homesteads again. Take their wagons and horses and hay—everything they've taken from you or destroyed. Leave them nothing but a day to remember."

He straightened up, lifted his reins. "One more thing: No drinking. This is going to call for clear heads and steady guns if we carry it off. We're not out to plunder the merchants or hurt the townsmen. We're not bandits after loot."

"But Russ," a man said in a protesting tone, "what you're talking about is a real war."

"There are only two ways we can fight them. Like we have been; a raid now and then; running off their stock, using their whips on them. That's one way. The other way is like this; attack them in force where it counts, crush them once and for all and end it. The first way will take a long time and cost us a lot of lives and property. The second way—the way they'd least expect us to act—will finish them or us, but it'll finish the range war and that's what we're out to do."

In only one or two faces was there instant acceptance and approval. The majority of squatters looked thoughtful, uneasy, or downright fearful. He gave them a few minutes to think, then he turned his horse.

"It's a long ride; let's go."

They followed, crowding down off the hilltop and spreading out across the range, a few fanning out instinctively as videttes. Early morning dew darkened the fetlocks of their horses. Up ahead Mahoney and Metzen rode with Russ, whose words were clipped and hard.

"Mahoney; you probably won't need more'n fifteen men to seal off the south end of town. When you get them stationed so no one can slip past, ride around the place and make sure the others are spaced on the prairie so riders can't get past them."

"Sure."

"Bill—get the telegraph line first. Be sure about that. If a message gets out and help comes for the cowmen, we'll be bottled up in Cornell."

"I'll make sure, don't worry about that. After I get the line down what do I do?"

"Make a circuit like Mahoney's going to do. Be plumb certain the men out on the prairie don't get so far apart someone'll slip past them. Make a strong roadblock on the north road. I don't think many'll try to get out that way—not when they see us coming—but make it good in case they try it. There's another thing; anyone coming *into* Cornell—let them pass. We don't want word to leak out for a day at least."

"Cowmen too?" Metzen asked.

Russ nodded. "Anyone; cowmen, travellers, anyone. We'll keep them inside once they're there, but we don't want riders coming up, seeing what's going on, then streaking it for help."

"Maybe we ought to send a couple of men to cut the

telegraph line near Houton Creek, too," Mahoney said.

"No; they'd fix it and wonder why it was cut. We can't patrol both towns. If we work this right, Cornell will be cut off. For how long depends on how good our surround is."

"How much time are we going to need? What do you figure to do when you're inside the place?"

"I want the ringleaders like Bennett and Enright. I want their hostage. How much time it'll take to knock sense into them depends on how good our surround is and how much we impress them with our strength. Maybe a few hours, maybe all day. The longer it takes the worse our chances of success are, but I'll tell you one thing, there're going to be some damned surprised cowmen in Cornell today."

Metzen's face looked troubled. "Russ; you'd better get your mother first thing. Men who'd brand a kid would kill a woman."

"I know," Russ said, watching the brassy sun glimmer over the flawless distance. "Ride down the line Bill and pick out the ten best men with guns to stay with me when I ride into town."

Metzen looked around. "Ten? Are you going to ride into Cornell with only ten men?"

"The less I take the stronger our surround'll be, Bill. We can't afford to risk anyone slipping past us and we don't have enough men to storm the town and surround it too."

"But hell," Mahoney put in, "ten men—"

"Ten'll be enough," Russ said shortly. "When they see how many are around the town, I think the wise heads'll be against starting a war."

"Well," Mahoney said dubiously, "I hope you're

right. After I get the surround set up, I'll ride in, too. All right?"

"All right."

Mahoney drew aside and rode back among the squatters. Bill Metzen stood in his stirrups straining to see Cornell. He dropped back against the cantle finally and said: "I'd better head out now, find the line and cut it." He smiled. "See you in Cornell."

By the time Morgan's Men came in sight of Cornell, the ten gunmen were riding with Russ. Dust arose under their horses' hooves, the conversation which had been lagging for some time now, died altogether. Russ halted briefly and watched three distant riders snaking their way towards some slender poles set at intervals northward from the town. No one spoke until the men converged upon one pole, dismounted and went to work. The pole swayed under one man's weight and just for a second the sunlight flashed out along a quivering wire. When it parted and fell away, several squatters cheered.

When the band moved on again, the sun was high overhead. Time seemed to hang suspended. Moments went by, but not hours. It was as though the daylight were fixed in place forever.

Closer to Cornell the crowd of grangers met travellers. Russ ordered them taken along. There were some protests but mostly the captives were white-faced and silent; there were several cowboys among them.

Once more the squatters halted. Mahoney and a hard-riding swarm of men looped far out and around Cornell heading southward. Russ watched them go with warm satisfaction. So far, everything was moving precisely and efficiently. When he saw Bill Metzen waving his hat from the distance, he passed the order for all but his ten gunmen to break away for the surround. Half went west, half towards the east, or rear of Cornell. It was as though the squatters were practised at capturing towns. There was a thrill to the sight for Russ and his ten remaining men. From far ahead a shout drifted up to them from the town. When the dust-devils had settled and he could see the completed squatter-cordon, Russ continued towards Cornell. He watched the buildings grow larger, stand out against the flatness of the land, and the years of planning, of being lonely and apart, of schooling himself for this day, crowded into his mind. The suffering and sadness grew remote. In sharp perspective Cornell loomed as a symbol of what he had dedicated himself to destroy and the time was now! There was a cold sense of achievement deep in the remembering blood.

" Russ ? "

He turned his head. A heavily bearded man was pointing with a rigid arm towards the south, down where swirling yellow dust was settling in the wake of movement. There was a reflection of buggywheels. Farther back six riders were trailing the vehicle. The little entourage was heading straight for Cornell and while he watched, some of Metzen's men encircled the cavalcade. The buggy and riders slowed, drew down to a halt. Russ strained to see. Sunlight flashed off carbines when Metzen's men disarmed the men and waved them on into town.

Russ returned to his contemplation of the village. He was on the northern stage road between Cornell and Houton Creek and from his saddle he could see fairly well in all directions. For a time Cornell didn't seem to comprehend, then, slowly, men began to gather in the roadway. None attempted to ride out where the squatters were. They seemed dazed, unbelieving.

" All right," he said finally, " lay your carbines across your laps and let's go."

No one came out to oppose him. It was very still when he entered town ahead of his hard-looking companions. Men ducked quickly into saloons and stores. A few remained upon the plankwalks, staring. It was quiet enough to hear the slightest sound. From doorways, men and women watched him ride past. There was shock and fear in most faces. Three cowboys walked unexpectedly out of the liverybarn and stopped dead still, staring. One of the squatters reined up before them.

" Give me those guns."

He got them without a word, shoved them into his waistband and rejoined his friends without looking back. A soft sound, like a rippling sigh, followed in his wake.

Russ drew up in the thin shade before the Cattlemen's Club Saloon. When he dismounted the ten men got down and moved up closer. He jutted his chin at several of the men. " Patrol the plankwalks, boys. Whoever you see with a gun—take it. We don't want any shooting if we can help it. You two come with me. Now all of you keep your eyes open—from now on every second counts."

He entered the saloon, saw that he was expected from the unnaturally stiff postures of the men there, and thought that by now Cornell knew who he was and what was happening, how in times of strife, news travels with the speed of light. Men looked at him without speaking, without changing their expressions. It was so still, a blundering fly caught in a spider's web made enough noise to be heard a hundred feet away.

There were four men with their backs to the bar staring at him. Of the dozen or so patrons, they alone had the earmarks of gunmen. One of them was a two-gun man. By his flat hat, his inlaid, small-rowelled spurs, and his lean, merciless look, Russ knew him to be a Texan.

When Russ broke the hush, he directed his words to this man.

" Are you a rider for the Texas Company, mister? "

" I am," the gunman answered evenly. " And who the hell are you? "

" My name is Russ Morgan. Does that tell you anything? "

" Enough," the Texan said. " You got guts coming here."

" What's your name and how long've you been riding for the Company? "

" 'Name's Jack Smith and I've been with 'em long enough."

Russ crossed the room, stopped close to the Texan. His companions remained by the doorway. " If you're an old hand, Jack, maybe you'll know about a couple of killings last night."

" Maybe—maybe not. If you mean the old woman— I don't know nothing about that."

" You weren't in on that? "

" No."

" But you know where they've got her, don't you? "

" Nope."

Russ stood hip-shot, relaxed looking. " But you know how to handle a branding iron, don't you? "

" That wasn't me."

" But you were there."

" So were fifteen other fellers."

" Who used the iron? "

" I don't know."

Russ moved with startling speed. His fist caught the Texan high in the chest. He went down, careened off the bar and rolled over, doubled up and coughed. Russ bent, lifted him with one hand, held him close—too close for the Texan to use his guns.

" Who branded my brother? "

" I—don't—know."

Russ struck him again, let him fall into the sawdust again, bent, took his guns and tossed them backwards towards the door. The Texan made no attempt to get up. Russ turned slightly, faced the next gunman.

" You! Are you a Texas Company rider, too? "

The stranger had a little narrow head, which rode well back on his neck so that he had an appearance of looking down from a height. " No," he said quickly, " I'm an SB man. My name's Gordon and I wasn't anywhere around when them fellers hit the Morgan place."

" You weren't at the Tidd or Ashcraft place either, were you? Go ahead, Gordon, lie to me! "

The stain of guilt was on Gordon's face. " Listen, Morgan—"

" Why don't you try to draw, Gordon? "

" Listen; I do what I'm told. I get paid by SB."

" Does SB pay good for dead squatters? "

" You'd do the same for the—"

" How many other SBs are in Cornell today, Gordon? "

" I don't know. A few. I came in for the mail."

Russ's gaze was like still water. He beckoned with his head for the bearded man at the door—holding his cocked carbine now—to come closer. " Take this one outside. Tell the others to lock him up somewhere. We'll want him later." He watched the other faces as the SB rider was pushed towards the doors.

" The rest of you listen. Cornell is surrounded, the telegraph line is down. No one will come to help you and none of you can ride out. I'm here for some information. You just saw what happens to those who don't want to help, so make up your minds. I want to know where your people are holding Mrs. Morgan—the woman who was taken hostage night before last. I want the name of the man who branded those words on my brother's back. Speak up!"

For a moment there was utter silence. There were men among them who knew, Russ had no doubt about that. While he was gazing at them a man spoke out, he was ashen, with transparent sweat on his forehead and upper lip.

"Feller done that to your brother was Hen Catlett, a P-up-and-down rider."

"What's your name?"

"That don't matter. You asked a question and I answered it."

"Is Catlett in Cornell now?"

"I don't know. He was here this morning but I don't know about right now."

Russ nodded and said, "All right, mister; now you'd better come with us. Sounds like you're standing on the wrong side of the fence."

"No I ain't," the man said, dry-eyed and frightened. "I'm no squatter-lover. I got no use for them people."

"After what you just told me," Russ said, "you'd better come along. The squatters'll protect you. That's more'n your friends are going to do after this."

"I'll slope."

"Not out of Cornell you won't. If you don't want to come along then you'd better go into hiding. The cowmen'll have you killed for opening your mouth. What about the woman they took hostage?"

"I don't know nothing about that. None of us do. We heard they got her, but no one knows where they're holding her."

Several men entered the saloon. Russ looked into the back-bar mirror. One was Bill Metzen, the others were also squatters. He flicked a glance at the other men in the room.

" Let your guns drop, boys," he said. " Slow and easy now; so far no one's died. It'd be too bad if it started in here."

The guns dropped heavily. Bill and another man went forward to retrieve them. On his way past, Russ Metzen bent a little and spoke.

" The place is scared stiff, Russ."

" How's the surround? "

" Good. They've turned back quite a bunch trying to get out, so far. Mahoney's watching like a hawk. What's next? "

" I'll be with you in a minute." When Metzen went back by the door Russ studied the cowmen and townsmen. Of the lot, the weakest, most ineffectual looking one was the man who had named his brother's attacker. Somewhere, a long way off, a dog barked and a man cried out. Russ was tensed for the shot. It never came.

" You boys may have a lot of ideas," he told the saloon patrons, " but if you're smart, you'll stay right in here. Of course, if you're hell-bent to fight, why there're half a hundred squatters waiting outside to oblige you."

He backed towards the door and out through it. Metzen and the others moved after him. They followed him to another saloon. En route, Metzen passed out guns to the squatters they passed on the plankwalk. Inside, Russ asked the barman if Saul Bennett was in Cornell. The bartender said he didn't know if Bennett was still in Cornell, but he had been earlier.

"How about Forge Enright and Hewton Muller?"

"I don't know about them."

"Don't you?" Russ said gently.

The bartender's eyes grew fearful. "Morgan; don't put a man on the spot like this."

"You can feel sorry for yourself tomorrow," Russ said sharply. "Right now I want a straight answer—and quick—are any of them in town?"

"Muller and Enright are at the hotel. I know, because I was up there myself a little while ago—before I come on duty."

"Thanks." Russ cast a brief look at the three or four men sitting motionless along the wall. He made a gesture towards them and touched his own guns. A squatter went towards them.

CHAPTER 5

A Day To Remember

He stood on the plankwalk near the Cattlemen's Hotel, a large man wearing two guns in plain sight. No one called out to challenge him. After a moment's surveyal, seeing how the town was still and waiting, how the squatters were patrolling it with guns in their hands, he let his glance drift farther out. Cornell's cordon of sentries was clearly visible. Most squatted in the smashing sunlight beside their horses. There was no question, but that they fully intended to keep the town bottled up. The abruptness, the audacity, and the numbers of the squatters, plus a lack of leadership at the moment, deterred those among his enemies who might otherwise have taken their chances against Russ Morgan's guns.

With a beckoning jerk of his head he went up the rickety stairway of the Cattlemen's Hotel. Five men followed him. Among them was Bill Metzen. The sound of their passage was loud and sharp in the town's silence. A dingy corridor turned southward beyond the landing. Russ went down it without breaking his stride.

He went from room to room. Most were empty; three had pop-eyed occupants who looked up in startled wonder as the big man stared at them, then closed the doors without speaking. The fourth room held three men with guns in their laps and a terrible waiting in their faces. Of the three he recognised only one—Forge Enright.

" You've been a long time getting here, Morgan."

Metzen closed the door behind the last of the squatter gunmen. The room seemed chokingly close and stifling. Without looking away from Enright, Russ told the others to wait in the hallway. Metzen breathed a protest, got no answer and reluctantly went out with the others. When the door closed, Russ spoke.

" Where is she, Enright? "

" Not in Cornell, I'll tell you that much."

" Where? "

Enright's steady eyes grew cold and hard. " You won't find out from me."

Russ leaned upon the door. He paid no attention to the other two men. It was obvious what Forge Enright was doing. He still had his hostage, and while Morgan's strategy had taken him totally unawares, he still held a good hand.

" Well . . . ? " he said, when Russ remained silent.

" You're wrong, Enright, dead wrong. I'm here to find her—and a man named Hen Catlett. I'll find them."

" Will you; how? "

The man on Russ's left arose from his chair with a fluid movement. His gun was low and menacing. He opened his mouth to speak, but Enright cut in swiftly.

" Sit down. Don't be a fool. He knows nothing."

Russ swivelled his glance a little, raked the stranger with it and spoke. " That's the same as telling me you're Catlett, mister."

" Sit down! "

" Shut up, Forge," Catlett said from the corner of his mouth. " I don't need your advice. All right, Morgan, I'm Catlett; what're you going to do about it? "

" You must be pretty slow with that gun to have to hold it in your hand all the time, Catlett."

" You want to find out how slow? Just make a move, Morgan. You'll find out."

Russ said, " All right," and he was moving when he spoke, sideways and ahead, in long, wide strides. Two guns exploded simultaneously. A third shot rattled the windows and Russ spun with both guns bucking. The second man went off his chair sideways with two slugs in him, one in the head. Hewton Muller was dead.

Forge Enright had made no move to lift the gun in his lap. Henry Catlett was sprawled on the threadbare carpet. Enright glanced briefly at him, longer at Hewton Muller, then looked up, pale, flinty eyes unmoving. He spoke into the fragment of silence, which followed the explosions.

" You've avenged your brother, Morgan. I don't know

why Catlett waited. He was going to shoot you when you came through the door. I don't know why he waited."

"Why are you waiting, Enright?"

"I'm not going to match draws with you. I don't have to. You're fast. Those shots went off together, but Hen had the drop on you. I don't have to match you, Morgan. I don't even have to try."

"Who is the other one?"

"Hewton Muller—P-up-and-down."

Russ holstered his guns and stretched out one hand. "Give me that gun."

Enright passed it over just as several squatters burst into the room, guns drawn and cocked. Enright glanced at them briefly, then flicked his gaze to Russ again. He began to fill his pipe as calmly as though two dead men weren't within reach of him.

Russ handed Enright's gun to Bill Metzen without speaking. The squatters looked dazedly at the downed men, then up at Russ. Enright broke the silence.

"You're a regular hell-roarer, Morgan. I don't think I ever saw a faster gun. What good's it going to do you?"

"It settled up a score for my brother," Russ said.

"Yes," the cowman said cryptically but unruffled, "it did that, but that wasn't what made you try to take Cornell. We both know that."

"I didn't *try* to take it—I *took* it. Your hired killers didn't even challenge me, Enright."

"That's not important. You want my hostage, don't you? Well; you can have her as soon as you pull out and agree never to come back."

"I had you pegged for a bigger man than that, Enright. Only a coward would—"

"No; the only coward among us was Muller, and you

killed him. He stayed in town today because he's been trying to talk me into letting your mother go. You killed the wrong man, Morgan. You should've killed me and let Muller live. He was scared of you and I'm not. Especially when I've got the whip hand."

"You don't have as good a hand as you think, Enright. I'll get it out of you where my mother's hidden. It may take a little branding on the bottoms of your feet, Indian style, but I'll get it out of you."

A squatter came up and drew Bill Metzen to one side. Afterwards Bill looked at Enright first, then at Russ. "Some of the boys're holding a girl downstairs. They say she's quite a handful after hearing those shots."

"What about her?"

"She wants to see you, Russ."

"I don't want to see her." Russ turned back towards the Texas Company's senior partner. Enright had undergone a complete and swift change after Metzen's words. He was looking from Russ to Bill and back again. The iron harshness was gone from his face. Russ was puzzled for only a moment. When it dawned on him who the girl was, he seized upon an idea.

"Bill? I changed my mind. Send her up here. I guess you other fellers better drag those carcasses out of here before she comes up." He twisted up a cigarette while he was waiting, popped it in his mouth and lit it. Forge Enright watched each movement hypnotically. His mouth was locked in a grim slit.

When Bill returned Russ swung slightly to see the girl It was Diane Enright. Her taffy-coloured hair, sunburnt several shades of blonde, was drawn up at the base of her neck. She stopped just inside the room and stared unbelievingly at her father. Russ couldn't help but notice the similarity between them, even when neither looked natural. She went beside Enright's chair and swung to face Russ.

"You murderer!" she said in a tight, low voice, a winteriness showing in her eyes.

Forge said, "Diane; be quiet."

She ignored him. "Do you think you can get away with this? You must be insane—attacking a town like this. Over in Houton Creek I didn't take you seriously I didn't think you were this unbalanced."

"Diane!"

She stopped speaking with her lips still parted. Russ gazed at her, feeling neither anger nor resentment. He sensed the way her father was looking up at him.

"Well, Enright?"

"I don't understand."

"Like hell you don't. You were so full of confidence before she came up here. How do you feel now?"

Enright didn't answer.

"I suppose now you're ready to trade one hostage for another, aren't you? This visit shot your royal flush all to pieces, didn't it?"

Still silence.

"You have one minute to make up your mind."

"And if I refuse?"

Russ shrugged, kept his eyes on the older man's face. "That's no problem—no trade, no daughter."

"What do you mean, Morgan?"

"Refuse to trade and find out." He began to twist up another cigarette. "One minute, Enright. When this cigarette is half smoked your time is up." He lit it and raised his eyes to Diane Enright's face and was shocked by the hatred there. He felt an inexplicable need to explain.

"This isn't my doing, ma'm. I didn't ask for this range war."

"That's not true. I told you what would happen when we met at Houton Creek. You did this whole thing purposefully."

"Did I burn out squatters and whip them off? Did I gut-shoot animals and kill men in their fields? Did I—?"

"You hate so deeply you can't rationalise. The kind of hate that shows in your eyes, Mister Morgan, is the kind which destroys people. It will destroy you."

"Never mind me. I've been threatened before. What other way can the grangers keep what is theirs?"

"By obeying the law; by using tact when it comes to grazing their animals on the cowmen's range."

"Whose range? The cowmen don't own it. They never *did* own it. And you don't know what you're talking about; those people don't have any livestock left to turn out. If they did they wouldn't turn them out. They aren't stockmen, they're farmers; they believe in fences, in keeping what's theirs inside their own boundaries, on their own land, under their own fences. Obey the law? Cowman law? Where's the law in Cornell right now? I'll tell you; it's hiding, that's where it is, hiding so's it won't have to accept any complaints from squatters. That's where it's been for years now—avoiding homesteaders. If that wasn't so, Miss Enright, there wouldn't be any range war now."

"Even if that was true," she shot back at him, "you people still would have no right to take the law into your own hands."

"Is there another way?"

"The Army, the Federal authorities."

He made a snorting sound. "Cowman talk." He

glanced out of the window. In the distance were specks which were men beside their horses. " Come over here," he said to her, and preceded her to the window. When she was close he caught the faintest scent of lavender. For a fraction of a second his mind closed down upon the smell, savoured it, then he raised his arm and pointed.

" See those men? There isn't a one of them that hasn't tried to go to the law some time or another. Nothing ever came of it except more abuse. Don't you think they have limits just like anyone else? Listen; how would they get the Army here—by telegraph? Where is the telegraph office? Right here in the cowman's town of Cornell. What would happen if the cowmen heard a squatter had sent for help? "

" That's not so," she said. " They could ride after the Army."

" And leave their families unprotected? "

" Or go to Houton Creek—telegraph from there."

" And have it intercepted by Cornell's telegrapher? Miss Enright, this is cow country. You should know that better than anyone else. Those squatters have been scared so long—"

" But what is all this to you? " She turned and looked straight up at him.

" I told you once before. Cowmen killed my father. That was a long time ago."

" Can't you forget it? "

He stared down into her face. " Could you? " he said. When she turned, continued to gaze out of the window, he said. " Did you ever see a boy branded? "

" A what? "

" A young boy branded across the shoulders with a running iron."

" I never heard of such—"

"Diane," Forge Enright said. "Don't talk to him. Come over here."

Russ trailed her across to her father's chair. He looked significantly at his cigarette. It was more than half smoked. Enright watched him gauge its length and his nostrils quivered a little.

"Your time's up, Enright."

The Texas Company's man didn't speak. His head was averted and Russ could see only the craggy, hard profile. He turned and called for Metzen.

"Here, Bill," he said when the shorter man entered. "Two more hostages for you. How about the jail?"

"Good idea. The sheriff's already in there—along with some others who got ideas." Metzen studied Russ's face a moment. "Why don't you trade one woman for another?"

"I offered to. Enright's stubborn."

Diane looked at her father then up at Russ. She had a bewildered expression. "What are you talking about—trade one woman for another?"

Russ shrugged. "I'll let your father tell you about that. Maybe he can explain about the branded boy, too. I guess you'll understand those things as being necessary, being from the stock you are. You can have them Bill," he said, throwing down the cigarette, not lifting his face until both Enright's were gone.

Time; it was slipping past. He squinted at the sun. He hadn't wanted to get the information from Enright by force, especially after Diane came up.

Enright had said his mother wasn't in Cornell. If that was so, and he'd bet a good horse Forge Enright wouldn't lie to save his soul, then those guarding his mother wouldn't know what was happening at Cornell. It was a reassuring thought because it meant he had a little leeway as far as time was concerned.

He went to the door, past it to the stairway and started down. Several large men fell in silently behind him. He stopped part-way down and told the squatters to bring Hen Catlett along. They lugged the body out into the sunlight. Russ motioned for them to take it into the Cattlemen's Club Saloon. Grunting under Catlett's weight, the grangers pushed past the swinging doors, were greeted with stony silence, and put the body down.

Russ gazed at the patrons. There were several in the room who had not been there before. The wispy Texan named Jack Smith was not there, neither was the SB rider named Gordon.

"Recognise him, boys? Catlett, the man who branded my brother."

No one spoke.

"You there; you weren't in here before. What's your name and who do you work for?"

"'Name's Houston. I'm a P-up-and-downer."

"Your boss is dead," Russ said, and watched their eyes widen. He let it hang there a moment. "Houston; where have they got Mrs. Morgan?"

"I don't know—sir; I just went—"

"Russ! Russ!"

Burt Lavender came bursting through the doors. "Russ! Someone's fired the town!"

"What?"

"At the south end. Someone fired a shack down there. Now there's half a dozen burning."

Lavender's face was alive with excitement. Metzen whirled out of the doorway and Russ heard men shouting. He swore, swung his arm towards the men along the bar. "Some of you take these fellers to the jailhouse and lock them up." He crossed the room in giant strides and went outside, across the plankwalk out into the middle of the road. By then the smell of burning wood was strong in the late afternoon air. A man trotted by. He hailed him.

" Get your horse. Go out and tell Mahoney not to let a single man leave the surround."

" The fire . . ."

" I know, but we can't let up to fight it or they'll get out of town."

" The whole damned shebang'll go up, Russ."

He was swinging away when he replied. " Not if the cowmen fight it, she won't. Go tell Mahoney! "

Bill Metzen came running up, caught up to Russ in front of the jail. " It's spreading fast, Russ."

" Round up the townspeople; drive them down here. Organise a bucket brigade. I'll have Enright send the cowboys down."

Metzen hurried away. Russ cast a final look southward. While he looked a wild sheet of flame burst skyward. Thick, oily black clouds billowed in its wake. He thought it was someone's store of coal oil, wrenched open the door of the sheriff's office and thrust himself inside. The room was close and stuffy. Several squatters with guns looked up as he entered. Across the room were two strap-steel cages. Forge Enright and his daughter shared one with a dozen rough looking cowboys. The other cage was jammed with men. Before Russ could speak the outer door was flung violently inward and a fat man in a white apron shouted: " The town's afire! Sheriff; we got to . . ." the words died out. The fat man blinked around, then scuttled away. A squatter went to the door, sniffed, looked out, stiffened and stared southward. The fire's odour filled the room. Men looked at one another in amazement.

Russ crossed to Enright's cell and called for the key. When the door was unlocked he beckoned the cowman outside. Diane started forward also and while Russ was hesitating, she swept past him.

"Enright; someone fired the town southward where all those shanties are."

"Fired it?" Enright said incredulously. "Damn those squatters. You did—"

"Shut up and listen. It's going to take every man in Cornell to get the thing under control. I'll send the squatters who're in Cornell, but all the rest of the fighters will have to come from the townsmen and the cattlemen."

"What do you want me to do?"

"Take these men here and every other mother's son you can round up and go down there and fight fire."

"How about your men beyond the town?"

"They're going to stay beyond the town. None of you will be allowed to ride out. Remember that. Now get this, Enright; I'm holding you personally responsible for every man I turn loose from this jail. Every man."

Russ didn't await Enright's reply, but unlocked both cells and motioned the prisoners out. "Go with Enright," he said, "and the first one doesn't do what he's told will have me to answer to. All right, Enright—get going."

When the room was empty, Russ stood with his back to the cells gazing out of the door where the crackling of fire and the shouts and curses of men were intermingled. Perspiration was running under his shirt. Who would have done such a stupid thing; a squatter? It would probably never be known. Surely there were squatters bitter enough to fire Cornell. There might even be cowmen that—

"Mister Morgan."

He turned on the balls of his feet. Blinked at her. " I forgot you," he said.

" Can I help? "

" I don't see how."

" Then I suppose you'd better lock me up again." She half turned from him, paused a moment then faced him again. " What is it going to take to stop all this? What can I say to you that will make you come to your senses? Can't you understand you're only making things worse for everyone? Please, Mister Morgan, don't destroy *everything*."

" Well; *I* didn't start that fire. I don't know anything about it."

" Who did? There never was a fire in Cornell before."

" You really think I had it set, don't you? "

" Yes; that's exactly what I believe, but that isn't what I'm concerned with right now. I'm *begging* you to stop this war. I'm not arguing with you about it—I don't want to argue about it—all I want is for you to stop it."

" I'm going to stop it. That's why we came to Cornell today; to stop a range war. I can't stay here talking, Miss Enright." He went to the door, opened it and gazed back at her. " Give me your word you won't leave this room? "

" You have it."

He went outside, turned south and was several doors down from the jail when a man stepped out from between two buildings, raised a pistol and fired pointblank. Russ took the slug hard. He felt shock seal away the pain in his lower body and lunged at the assassin.

They went down in a clawing scuffle. The gunman was half Russ's size, but he fought like a bobcat, twisting, biting, panting and striking out blindly with his clubbed gun. Russ rolled with the blows, ducked under the pistol, groped for the man's throat with both hands and when he found it, bore down hard and held on until the assassin's resistence grew weak and futile; then he eased off and stared at the face. A shadow fell across it. Russ swung his head quickly. Mahoney was standing there with his gun out and his lips curled back from the teeth.

"He'd do that for the damned reward. For that lousy money."

Russ got stiffly to his feet, hobbled to the front of a store and leaned upon it while examining his leg. The bullet had sliced through his thigh in an angling way. It bled some, but the wound was a clean one, although painful.

"He ain't dead, Russ. Want me to finish him off?"

"No; take the gun and leave him there."

Mahoney went closer and bent from the waist. "Is it bad?"

"No, not bad, but it hurts. How come you to be in town?"

"Bill came out and relieved me. He told me about the fire and not to break the surround to fight it. Is that what you ordered?"

"Yes; there're enough folks in town to put the thing out. What I'd like to know is how it started."

"I think I know," Mahoney said. "Just before it started, we sent eight cowboys on into town. Right after that the fire commenced."

"That doesn't sound reasonable, Mahoney. Why would eight cowmen start a fire in their own town?"

"I don't know, but one of them was Bennett of SB, and I can tell you this about him—nothing's beneath him. If he thought a fire might divert us—or you—long enough for him to get away, he'd burn up his own mother."

" Where was Bennett the last time you saw him? "

" Bennett? I just came from the jailhouse. I locked him up in there. But say, Enright's daughter was—"

" I know. All right, Mahoney; go on down and help with the fire. I'm going back and talk with Bennett. By the way, as soon as it's possible to send Enright back up here, have a couple of the boys bring him along. But no hurry—make sure the fire's under control first."

Mahoney nodded and resumed his way southward. The assassin still lay unconscious, half on, half off, the plankwalk. Russ wondered again if Mahoney didn't know him, then retraced his way towards the sheriff's office. It pained him to walk and blood ran down his leg and into his boot, but the knowledge of the extent of his injury lessened its hurt in his mind.

The hurtling shadows of summer twilight were fast lowering. The smell of curing grass was saturated with a more pungent odour, and between them, they made sweat run in rivulets under Russ's shirt.

When he entered the jail a wizened man glared at him over twin barrels of a stubby scattergun, but only for a second, then he straightened up and mumbled an apology.

" Mahoney told me to stay here."

" Good. Bring Saul Bennett out."

" Man; you been hurt."

" A flesh wound. Get Bennett."

The guard tucked his riot-gun under one arm and swaggered to the cages with a ring of keys. He was grinning evilly, and wide enough to crack the crusts of tobacco juice at the outer corners of his mouth.

Russ sank into a chair with sweat criss-crossing his face.

He probed the wound, felt its swollenness and how the blood had stopped, and leaned back. When he looked up, Bennett was standing before him. There was a livid welt across the cowman's face as though from a quirt freely swung. His eyes were irate and afraid, both.

"Why'd you fire the town, Bennett?"

"Me? I don't know what you're talking about."

"You were seen," Russ said with a blank face. "What'd you expect to gain by it—a getaway?" When Bennett didn't answer Russ gestured to the wizened guard. "Take this man and those others with him, and turn them over to Mahoney down at the fire. Tell Mahoney to make them work twice as hard as anyone else. Tell him if they slow up to rawhide them a little."

"Be proud to." The squatter nudged Bennett ungently with his shotgun. "Get over yonder by the door —you!"

"Hey, guard," Russ called out. "Where's the girl?"

"I locked her in the other cell—with the sheriff."

"What sheriff? There wasn't any sheriff in here twenty minutes ago."

"Yes there was; he said you sent him down to fight the fire but he come back."

"Well; bring him out too."

Diane came first. She faltered at sight of his bloody trouser leg, searched his face quickly, then moved closer. Behind her a red-faced, tall, very thin man stopped short and glowered. Russ motioned the girl to one side.

"You're the sheriff? What's your name?"

"Buff Calkins. Morgan, you'll never get away with this."

"Why didn't you stay down there and help with the fire?"

" I'm the law hereabouts. I don't take orders from no cussed squatters."

Russ got out of the chair slowly. He towered above the lawman. In a quiet voice he said, " Sheriff; if I go to work on you, you won't be able to fight fire or anything else for a long time. Do you want to go along with these other men or stay here and get used up a little? "

Calkins' glare wavered. After a moment he said, " I'll go, but by golly—"

" Shut up and get going."

Saul Bennett and the others moved out soundlessly. When the door closed behind them, Russ twisted to look at Diane Enright. Into the silence of the little room came the shouts and cries of men battling the fire. The bedlam made a strange and savage background for the long stare they exchanged, before she spoke.

" Did Mister Bennett really start the fire? "

" Did he deny it? "

She frowned and shook her head. " He must have done it accidentally—or because he thought it better to burn Cornell then let you plunder it."

" We're not plundering the place."

" I saw men taking horses and wagons."

" To replace things taken from them by your people, Miss Enright."

" That's jungle law."

" Call it what you want, it's the best kind in this country."

" Are you a judge? With a price on your head and a long list of murders behind you? "

" The cowmen put that price there because I wouldn't take their abuse without fighting back, and I've never murdered anyone in my life—never."

"My father told me about Henry Catlett."

"If he called that murder he's a liar. Catlett had his gun in his hand, aiming at me, when I shot him. Muller was behind me when he shot at me. Both men had a better-than-even break. That's not murder."

"The other stories——"

"Stories; what'd you expect the cowmen to say—the truth? If they told that it'd show *them* up, not me."

She regarded him steadily for a moment. "Every time we meet we argue."

"That's natural, we're on opposite sides of the fence."

"But that's possible without hating—without fighting. A lot of people have different beliefs, but they don't judge one another, kill and burn and plunder."

He flexed his injured leg. The pain had gone and in its place was a numbness. "Then don't judge me."

"I don't—except; well—the *way* you're fighting back isn't civilised; isn't legal or even decent."

"If that isn't judging me I don't know what is," he said.

"Well, it isn't, whether you think so or not. I *condemn* you, I don't judge you. You're mad; irrational with hatred. I've told you this before; that kind of fury will destroy you. For your own good and ours, you should be locked up until you come to your senses."

"So the cowmen can steal more women as hostages, brand more boys with running irons, bushwhack more squatters, burn them out? He got up shaking his head. "You talk about right and wrong—a cowman's daughter who doesn't *know* the difference."

"I don't believe those stories," she said, unperturbed in the face of his bigness and closeness, the increasing sharpness of his voice. "I think you've made those things up to influence the squatters against the cowmen."

"Ask your father; I have no use for him, but I don't

think he's a liar. Ask him what is true and what isn't."

"Even if those things were true," she said, "would two wrongs make a right?"

He was gazing very steadily into her face. "Turning the other cheek didn't work out so well, the squatters tried it for five years. All that came of it was a lot less cheeks to turn. Listen, Miss Enright; if you'd wanted to know the truth you'd have asked around. You wouldn't have shut your mind to what's been happening here since you and I were kids."

"Rumours, exaggerations."

"Dead men aren't rumours and burnt out homesteads aren't exaggerations. You haven't wanted to know, that's all. Your paw sent you away to school, bought you nice clothes, gave you money; you didn't want to believe it came from other men's sufferings. Money'll do that to folks. Well; no more, Miss Enright. I'm back to teach these horse-riding lords of the earth that after you slap the other cheek you'd better run for cover. Before I'm through I'll have your Texas Land and Cattle Company on its knees, I promise you that."

"You think you're above justice, don't you? You'd ruin the countryside out of hate, wouldn't you?"

He crossed the room without replying, swung open the cell door and jerked his head at her. "Inside."

"Now I'm a prisoner, too."

He didn't answer until she went past him and he was locking the door. "You put the worst meaning on everything. No, you're not a prisoner. I'm doing this because it's best. Before this day is over, it'll be dangerous for a girl to be loose in Cornell."

They looked at one another a moment, then she turned away.

CHAPTER 6

Vengeance!

Outside the dying day was warm, acrid, and dusky. The smoke was like a pale film. He looked up, sky-lining the town. There was no flame that he could discern.

" Russ? "

He turned. " Mahoney? Did you get the fire out? "

" All but the mopping up," Mahoney said. There was a sound of men and spurs in the gloom down the plankwalk behind him. " We've got thirty cowmen to lock up somewhere."

" Thirty? There weren't that many in town."

Mahoney made a grimace. " Well, there are now. That was behind Bennett's idea in firing the place. Cowmen'd see it from all over the range and come a-helling. They did—and rode right in to the surround. The boys cleaned 'em out right down to the skin and marched 'em on into Cornell. There're some hard ones among them, too, real gunslingers."

" Are those them down the road? "

Mahoney turned and beckoned. A bristling guard of squatters drove the prisoners forward. Saul Bennet was among them, dishevelled and worn-appearing.

Mahoney said, " What do you want done with them? "

" Lock them up inside and leave some men to guard them. Don't crowd the cell Miss Enright's in, though."

"Somebody hung one of them."

"What?"

"A big feller. Somebody caught him during the fire, belted his legs and arms and hung him." Mahoney shrugged. "No one saw it happen. I asked around, but couldn't find out anything much." As though acting on a hunch, Mahoney turned to Saul Bennett. "Did you recognise that feller, Bennett?"

"Yes, I recognised him. Buff Calkins—the sheriff."

"The hell," Mahoney said in surprise, and looked up at Russ. "I suppose most anyone could've hung the sheriff. He'd have plenty of enemies, even among the cowmen."

Russ looked over the heads of the prisoners. Tiny stars were beginning to glitter in the vast sweep of heaven, numberless, brittle, and cold looking. First Hewton Muller and Hen Catlett, now Calkins... He looked at Bennett but spoke to Mahoney.

"Take good care of that one, Mahoney, we'll want both of them alive—Bennett and Enright."

"Enright's still down there. He's sort of took over the bossing job. How's your hurt?"

"It's all right. Listen; after you lock these men up you'd better go down there and sort of guard Enright."

Mahoney shrugged. "What's another dead cowman," he said. "You said yourself we didn't have to give no quarter."

"To your enemies when you're fighting them, Mahoney, not to prisoners after you've disarmed them." He gestured towards the jailhouse. "Go on. Lock them up."

He stood aside and watched the shadowy figures slouch by. As Mahoney had said, there were some hard-looking men among them. All were unarmed and most of them had lost their shirts, boots, even their hats, to the squatters.

"Hey, Russ."

He watched the sturdy shadow advance until it assumed an identity; Bill Metzen. His lips were moist as though he had stopped somewhere for a long drink of water.

"How's the surround holding, Bill?"

"Like rawhide. That last bunch we sent in—"

"Mahoney's locking them up right now."

"Well; look here. One of the boys found this on one of them." Bill held out a much folded and soiled piece of paper.

Russ took it, twisted to catch some light and saw the likeness of a man staring at him from the centre of the page. The face was familiar. Reading the bold print he found that he knew the man; had, in fact, moon-lighted cattle with him in Colorado. "I'll be damned," he said.

Metzen nodded briskly. "Look at the size of that reward. One thousand dollars in gold coin, it says."

Russ started for the sheriff's office, entered and squinted against the fog of tobacco smoke filling the room. "Here," he said to a squatter. "Find a man in there named Flake Willis and bring him outside the front door. I'll be waiting out there to talk to him."

When Willis came Russ had sent Bill Metzen back beyond the town to maintain the surround and pass word the siege was going as well as could be expected.

"Howdy, Flake," he said softly when the outlaw stopped in front of him. "You're a long way from home."

The outlaw squinted, then rocked back on his heels. "So it *is* you. By golly, when I hired out down here I heard you was the leader of the squatters, but hell,

Russ..."

"Yeh; I know. For enough pay you'd—"

"Now you know a sight better'n that," Willis said genially. He was grinning raffishly.

"Forget it, Flake. You just signed on with the wrong side, that's all."

"It didn't look like that until tonight. Anyway, squatters never have enough money to hire guns; you know that; and a feller's got to eat."

"Or be eaten," Russ said. "It was foolish to pack that wanted poster around with you. The squatters not only know who you are, they know you're worth a thousand dollars to the Territory of Wyoming."

"I was kind of proud of that picture," the burly outlaw said. "'Course it was taken about ten years ago."

"Who hired you down here?"

"Fat guy named Muller."

"He's dead."

Flake Willis's eyes widened. "You do it?" When Russ nodded, the outlaw swore with feeling. "Who pays me now?" he asked.

"I guess you just don't get paid, Flake."

Willis looked thoughtful. "No sense in me hanging around then, is there?"

"A thousand dollars means a lot to these squatters. I don't think any of them ever saw that much money at one time in their lives."

"Ah, now, Russ..."

"They'd raise hell and prop it up if I turned you loose."

"You sure changed since those times in Colorado—"

"I haven't changed, Flake; it isn't that. Up there it didn't mean anything to me. I was just learning how to be as hard and fast as the best of them. What I'm doing down here is why I wanted to know those things. I came from here—those cowmen ambushed my paw. Now they've got my mother prisoner and one of them named Catlett used a running iron on my brother."

Willis's face screwed up. " You mean—branded him?"

Russ nodded. " I've been working up to this for the last few years, Flake; any cowman is my enemy down here—any hired gun . . ."

" Well, of course, I didn't know nothing about that, Russ. Why hell, you know me; if I'd known how the wind blew—"

" All right; you know now."

" Well, I'll just drop out, Russ. Hell; I wouldn't buy into no game against an old pardner—you know me better'n that. You know how it is—a feller takes the best pay he can get and makes a few sashays, shoots up a cabin or runs off a few head of stock, but he ain't really trying to hurt anybody. Nothing personal to it."

" What do you know about the things they've done, Flake? "

" The cowmen? I was out at one of their holding grounds the other night when a herd of those damn— when some of the squatters came swooping down and stampeded a bunch of cattle and shot hell out of the place. Outside of that I've only been along on a couple of hay-stack burnings."

" Any killings? Listen, Flake; I'm going to hold you until I find out, so don't lie to me."

" Honest, Russ—no killings. Muller—this feller I signed on with—he was sort of holding back. Those Texans and the SB were doing most of the real battling. In fact, it was the SB and the Texas Company who sent out raiders last night and killed a couple of squatters. We heard about that this morning. Our foreman was waiting for Muller to come back from town when one of the boys out on the range came bustin' in with news Cornell was afire. He brought us all down here together and you know the rest. We saw a long line of horsemen —thought they were SB or Texans, and when we rode up it was too late to get away. Those cussed sod-busters had us covered with more guns'n an army owns."

"All right," Russ said. "Let's go back inside. You're going to be locked up until I check on you. And Flake— for old times sake, I hope you haven't been in on any murders." He motioned with his head towards the door. "Keep quiet about knowing me. Don't tell the other cowmen anything at all, and if you turn out to be like you say, I've got a job for you."

He stood behind the outlaw and nodded towards the cell. One of the guards herded Willis towards it. Speaking aside to another squatter, Russ sent the man to find Forge Enright and bring him back to the sheriff's office. Before he closed the door and returned to the darkness under the sheriff's office overhang, he caught a glimpse of Diane Enright watching him.

Outside, he made a cigarette, lit it, exhaled and felt the swelling flesh where the assassin's bullet had ploughed. The skin was drawing tight, there was fever in it.

The night was down in earnest. A thin-bladed moon hung in the east. The heat was gone and in its place a benign coolness existed. He didn't know whether it was the wound, the night, or the sharply etched vision of slate-grey eyes staring at him in the back of his mind, but something had drained most of his tenseness away. He actually felt relaxed and drowsy.

Enright came up. Russ motioned the guard away.

Enright looked tired and exhausted. He was not a young man and the last six or seven hours had been a strain in many ways.

"Listen, Enright," Russ said, and was surprised at the mildness of his own voice, "if you've learnt your lesson, I'm willing to make peace. First off, I want my mother released and brought here. When I see her I'll give you back your daughter."

"Where is Diane?" Enright asked.

"She's safe."

"If you touch her Morgan, I'll fight you to hell and back."

"I guess you know how it feels to be on the other side, now, don't you? That's pretty low, taking your war out on women."

Enright leaned upon the building, grateful for the bulwarking support it gave him. He gazed doggedly across the deserted roadway.

"You're whipped, Enright. Muller's dead, Bennett's a prisoner, you've lost your town and before I'm finished here tonight you'll lose those top-notch gunmen you've paid so much money to bring in here."

"This fight is a long way from being over with, Morgan."

Russ dropped the cigarette, ground it out under a boot heel. "I said I was ready to make peace; I am; but I guess you aren't ready yet so I'll give you a last chance. Tell me where you've got my mother, or when I pull out of Cornell, Enright, I'll take your daughter with me."

"I'll hunt you down—"

"I'm not finished. When I ride out of town if this war isn't over, *I'll* fire the place, Enright, and burn it to the ground. There's another job I'll do, too. I haven't told your daughter how you've been fighting, Enright. She thinks that story about branding a boy's back and holding an old woman hostage are lies. I let her think so because I figured she'd ask you when both of you were in jail—I guess she didn't ask. That, or you didn't tell her—"

" You'd never get her to believe that, Morgan."

" Yes I could, because like I said—when I ride out of here I'll take her to my camp and show her my brother's back. He's still alive; I guess you didn't think he would be, did you? You thought he'd be dead like my other brother. What'll she believe about her father after she sees *that?* "

Enright's profile was a grey mask. He leaned there without speaking. Russ let the silence draw out for a while, then he turned, rapped on the jailhouse door and when a squatter peered out he asked to have Diane Enright brought out.

" Listen, Morgan," Forge Enright began. " You're fighting like a coyote. You're trying to destroy—"

" Who sent men to my folks' place? Who started this Indian style fighting? It wasn't me, Enright."

The door opened and Diane stood in the pale light peering into the darkness at them. When she recognised her father she moved quickly to his side, took his arm in both her hands and drew up closer to him.

" Diane—"

" I'll do the talking, Enright. Miss Diane; up there in the hotel I said something about trading one woman for another; do you recollect that? "

" Yes."

" And when I told you about branding a boy—you remember that, too? "

" Yes."

"I figured you'd ask your paw about them, that's why I didn't say more'n that. I wanted *him* to tell you. I knew you wouldn't believe me. You said you wouldn't."

"That was afterwards, Mister Morgan."

"It makes no difference," Russ said, and looked inquiringly at Forge. The older man's face was locked against the outside world; he was not going to speak. "I guess it's time you got the truth. To start with, your people—the cowmen—went out to the Morgan place a couple of nights ago—"

"Looking for you," she said.

"No, they weren't looking for me at all. They went out there to take hostages—my mother and two brothers. Your paw figured if he had my family he could force me to quit fighting. One of my brothers tried to defend the place. They killed him; somebody shot him in the head after he was dead. Your people took my other brother out into the yard—and made my mother watch—while they branded him across the shoulders with a red-hot running iron."

Her face was pale. She flickered a quick look at her father. He was like stone.

"They branded two words—Just Begun—on his back. Those are the same words your father said to me the last time we met; when he offered me twenty thousand dollars to leave the country and never come back. They meant he was just beginning to fight me. Now then—if I'd told you this any other way you'd have said it was a lie. All right; here's your father—go ahead and ask him if I'm lying, and if he says I am I'll take you out where my brother is and show you his back. Go ahead, Miss Diane; ask him."

But she didn't. She continued to hold her father's arm,

but more as a support than as a symbol of affection, and looked away from them both for a moment.

"Well?" Russ said. "You can't be so cold, things like that don't mean something to you."

"Please ... it's sickening." She faced Russ with a liquid stare. "But you don't *want* to understand. You *won't* understand. I believe you; I think I suspected something like this up at the hotel, but as terrible as these things are, they aren't the most important things."

"No?' Russ said bitterly. "Aren't they?"

"You're both wrong—terribly wrong. You can't keep this up. It'll bleed the country dry. Neither of you are the law. You're not justice, you're men. You're equally to blame. Dad; you've always thought because there wasn't much law out here, there was reason to rule with might—but that's wrong. There's human decency here. Might isn't right.

"Mister Morgan; hatred has warped you. You aren't normally a killer, a gun. You've gone to the extremes like my father has. You're both destroying the very things you're trying to keep alive. Dad's ruining the Company, bleeding it poor to hire gunmen, to keep big crews around to burn out squatters, not to work the cattle. And you—you're leading those same squatters against men who've been using guns since they were children. If you don't stop, Mister Morgan, after what's happened in Cornell today, every time a cowman sees a squatter—or a squatter sees a cowman—one or the other will be killed. When it's all over there won't be anything left but the gunmen. The squatters will be ruined and so will the cowmen."

"And my dead brother—my father?"

"The cowmen have lost men, too. Can't you see—

both sides have to forget. If you live for revenge you'll die because of it—both of you. Before you die you'll ruin everyone else; Mrs. Morgan, the other widows, their children; the cowmen's families..."

"Morgan," Forge Enright said suddenly without looking at either of them, "you keep bringing up your father. I'll tell you this—the man who killed him is dead."

"Who?"

"Buff Calkins."

"You know Calkins killed my father?"

"I know it."

"You sent him to do it?"

"No; no one sent him to do it. He came riding into Cornell looking for a job. The cattlemen's association told him they needed a sheriff, but they'd only hire one who knew how to treat squatters. Calkins said he'd show us he knew how—and when he came back later, he told us what's he'd done. I won't say we weren't in favour of it, but none of us told him to do it."

"Do you know who hung Calkins?"

"No. All I know is that someone did. I saw him being cut down. What I'm telling you is that the man who killed your father was not authorised to kill him, and somehow, probably without suspecting it, the men who lynched him made him pay with his life for your father's murder."

"And my dead brother...?"

"I don't know who did that. I can find out, but remember, Morgan, that lad was shooting at *them*, too. He killed one, in fact."

"And my mother, Enright?"

There was bleak silence, broken finally by Diane " I'll bring her to you, Mister Morgan. I'll find her and bring her to Houton Creek and send word to you."

He was looking at her father when he spoke. " Do you think you can? He hasn't told me, and I've promised to pull down his world unless he does."

" Just trust me," she said. " Believe in me. I'll bring her to you. We've got to start trusting some time ... I won't offer to trade with you, but I'll ask you to take your men out of Cornell and I'll find her for you; bring her to you. Just take your squatters out of town—no fires, no more killing. Give me your word and I'll give you mine." On an impulse she held out her hand.

He stood for a moment in total silence. " I don't see how you can do it," he said finally.

Her hand dropped away. She said nothing.

" As soon as we ride out of here *they'll* get organised again." He gazed at her father. " Enright; if you'll ..." the older man's granite profile was unheeding. Russ looked away from it to Diane. " It's no use," he said.

She moved swiftly around her father, caught Russ by the arms and held him so earnestly he could feel the bite of her fingernails. She was close to victory and knew it.

" One of you has to make the first concession. If he won't then you must ..."

She said a lot of things and he heard them, but the straining whiteness of her face, animated with conviction, was the most real thing to him. He raised his arms to touch her, caught her hands and held them and let her rush of words run together in his mind until she stopped speaking, stood still and motionless looking up at him. And he nodded.

" Promise me one more thing; when you find her, *bring* her to me, don't just send her."

" I will."

He released her hands and turned towards Enright.
" Don't try to stop her, Forge," he said. " Don't make
any trouble for her."

Enright had turned, was looking at his daughter. If a
face can age in moments his had, but perhaps it was only
the tiredness that dulled his sharp eyes and let the cheeks
sag.

Mahoney came out of the sheriff's office and teetered
on the threshold looking at the trio. Russ nodded and
Mahoney walked over where they stood in the gloom. He
looked inquiringly at Russ.

" The place seems quiet," Russ said.

" By now I expect most townsmen are abed," Mahoney
said.

" Did the fire do much damage? "

" Its share. If it'd gotten away from the shanties it'd
have burnt the whole place down." Mahoney bobbed
his head in Forge Enright's direction. " He strung his
boys out like he knew what he was doing."

Russ didn't look at Enright. " We're riding out," he
said. " Take a horse and go tell Bill to have his men
ride on in."

" You satisfied? " Mahoney asked. " You got your
mother? "

" No, I haven't got her—but she'll be safe."

Diane Enright moved to speak. Russ caught her hand
in the dark and closed his fingers around it. She shot
him a glance and remained silent. Mahoney turned away.
After he was gone she spoke.

" Why didn't you tell him? "

" No need," he said. " Those men don't question me,
ma'm, but if you'd said what really happened, they'd start
the trouble all over again. They feel pretty hard about

her being taken as a hostage. The fire's died down now, in more ways than one; let's not stir it up again." He let go of her fingers. " That's how you want it, isn't it?"

" Yes. I didn't understand. I'm sorry."

" I ought to take your father back with me . . ."

" No; if you did that it would be the same as telling the squatters about your mother. The cowmen would have another reason to continue the fighting."

" We're allies against both sides, aren't we?" he said.

" If *we* can be successful, the others can," she said. " But someone's got to show them how."

" And if this doesn't work—what then?"

" It's got to work; it's *got* to."

He touched Forge Enright lightly on the arm. " In case it doesn't," he said, " I want you to know I've got an ace in the hole. Those years I was away, Enright—I spent them in the north country in pretty hard company. If you begin this war over again, I pass you my word, I'll have fifty *real* gunslingers down here in five days. When I ride into Cornell next time, it'll be to burn the place to the ground and hang every man-jack I can catch. I'm not bluffing."

They heard the whooping riders coming along before they burst into Cornell from all directions. Bill Metzen and Mahoney rocketed up in front of the sheriff's office in a dark swirl of dust. Metzen threw a long, unpleasant look at Forge Enright, dismounted and grinned at Russ.

" Bill says it's all over."

" That's right."

"How about him," Metzen said with a jerk of his thumb. " Has he had enough?"

" Yes, he's had enough."

" In that case how about the fellers who've been out on

the surround sort of finding a few wagons and what-nots for themselves; the boys you kept in town seem to have done right well."

"Go ahead," Russ said. "You can have an hour. After that we're leaving."

Metzen hurried away with Mahoney just as the men in the jailhouse came out to see what the commotion was. Russ told them the siege was ended, the men from the prairie had come in, and they would all leave within an hour. They all began talking and shouting at once, gradually they drifted away in search of their friends. Some, who had never owned high-heeled boots before, teetered and swaggered to their own amusement, and the howls of their companions. All had at least one pistol and one carbine.

"Are you sure they won't start another fire or plunder the town?" Diane Enright asked.

"No, I'm not sure, but they were told before we rode in here they could take what they wanted from *cowmen*—not from anyone else. They aren't savages, ma'm, they're men who have had so little for so long all they ask is a chance to make good their losses." He made another cigarette, lit it and inhaled. "Enright; do you know who started that fire?"

"Yes, I know; he told me."

"Well, let me suggest something to you. Bennett isn't much; he rushes into things half-cocked, gets all worked up and gets to believing some of his own tall yarns. You can make him toe the line. You're the leader and I guess you always were. Keep SB in line; I know you haven't said you were through fighting but I think you are. I think you know you are, too. Don't let Bennett start anything, that's my advice to you, because, like I said before, if this thing flares up again, nothing—and nobody —is going to stop me from breaking the back of every cow outfit in the country. I'll bring in enough gunmen to do it without the squatters."

"What're you going to do with the men in jail?" Enright asked.

"Turn them loose. It'll be up to you to get rid of them. There's one I'm taking with me. His name's Flake Willis. He was a P-up-and-down rider. I knew him up north, so he won't be a hostage."

"Why are you taking him then?"

"Well; there's a price on his head and a few of the squatters know about it. We used to be friends in Colorado. Flake is a good man with a gun, but not really dangerous. I'm going to send him north with word to round up all our old friends and await word from me. 'You understand what I'm getting at?"

"I understand."

Russ turned to Diane. "You'd better let me send a couple of men with you, when you get ready to ride. Maybe it'd even be better if I left a—"

"No; no one'll bother me alone, but if I had squatters with me they might."

"How are you going to work it?"

"Well—I don't think I should tell you right now. You wouldn't tell your plans, would you?"

"No, I guess not. How long is this going to take?"

"Not very long. Probably not more than a few hours —a full day at the most."

Russ blinked. "You must have a pretty good idea."

"I have," Diane said, "and you said you'd trust me."

He half smiled at her. "Seems strange how hard we were hating each other two hours ago, ma'm."

CHAPTER 7

Aftermath

He led the squatters out of darkened Cornell with a smell and foretaste of winter in the night air. He thought it wouldn't be long before the driven blizzards would come screeching out of the high country again. Then there would be the thaws and high, impassable waters; the mud, the white-breathed frost and killing cold.

He thought of that and other things, but uppermost, he thought of Diane Enright's sincerity. He hoped with all his spirit she could produce, and perhaps sway her father, like Russ and the squatters had not been able to do, despite the ruin and force they brought against him. He thought also that it wouldn't have bothered him much to have badgered Enright into a gunfight and killed him. The cowman's iron-headedness lingered in his mind as something to be humbled.

There was comfort in the thought that he and the squatters had broken the power of their enemies, though, for no matter what Enright and Bennett said or did now, a great many of their hirelings would desert them. It was one thing to intimidate homesteaders who cringed, quite another thing to face up to a small army of men ready and willing to fight any odds.

It was over. It was over *if* Diane brought his mother safely to the camp. He willed that she would succeed, because the look in her face, the things she had said to him, were honest things; true things. If they resumed the range war, the only ones who would ultimately triumph, were the gunmen, as she had said.

They didn't make the camp until shortly before dawn. Up there his brother was waiting. There were several others, too; the old man who tended Will's injury, several of the riders who had been out with Mahoney on the cattle drive; men either unfit or too worn out, to participate in the attack upon Cornell.

The band off-saddled in weary silence, turned their horses out and sought their blankets. Until noon of the following day they would continue to straggle in, for many were driving wagons while others had pack animals in tow. Will's companion made Russ another dish of stew and had it ready when the older brother dropped down upon the ground near the younger man. Will had a wide and questioning look. He waited while Russ ate and drew an evil-smelling saddleblanket around his shoulders.

"You look pretty used up, Russ."

"I am. We all are."

"Tell me about it."

Russ propped himself against a tree and watched the faint-bracing light quickening in the east. There was an immense mountain far off, a little apart from other mountains on the horizon, and the sun brightened its face and tinted it pink, but for all its freshness, there was something melancholy in the scene.

"We took Cornell, Will. We surrounded it and cut the telegraph wires. All afternoon and until pretty late, we kept anyone from leaving the place." He looked into his brother's face and saw the lines scored deeply there by suffering. "Mother wasn't there."

"You didn't find her?"

"No; but I think she might be along tomorrow."

"Is she hurt, Russ?"

"No. Forge Enright's daughter's going to find her and bring her here."

Will's eyes were still. "She's the real pretty girl. I've seen her a few times. I heard she was living over at Houton Creek with an aunt, or something like that. So she knows what they did with maw."

"Not exactly. She asked me to wait a day or so longer and let her find maw and bring her to us up here."

"But her paw'll skin her alive."

Russ made no answer.

Will said, "Tell me all of it. Was there much fighting?"

"None at all, to speak of. We came down on them too suddenly. I guess Cornell was the last place they expected to see a band of squatters."

"No gunfights?"

"Well; one. I didn't hear of any others."

"Who got killed?"

"Hewton Muller of P-up-and-down, and a feller named Henry Catlett."

"Who was he?"

"The man who used the hot-iron on you, Will."

"Oh," the younger Morgan said in disappointment. "I didn't want him killed. I wanted to hunt him down by myself."

"It's better this way."

"Who killed him?"

"I did."

"Oh."

There was a depth of silence while they exchanged a long look, then Russ reached for his tobacco sack. "How's your back."

"It hurts, but it's a lot better. There'll be a scar."

"Yeah; can't get away from that, Will."

"You look plumb used up, Russ."

"I am. I could sleep for a year."

"What're you worrying about—maw?"

Russ nodded. "Yeah. Maybe I did the wrong thing, kid. I could've twisted it out of Enright, but after Diane showed up, I listened to her."

"What do you think he'll do?"

"That's it, Will, I don't know. He didn't talk much. He's as hard as iron—that old devil. I was in a hell of a spot. If I'd rawhided it out of Enright where he had maw—the girl'd have stuck by him—against me."

"But maw comes first, Russ. You—"

"Of course she does," Russ snapped. "But you see, somebody lynched that cowman-sheriff, and I was afraid if the boys found out that Enright was still full of fight and refused to tell where he had maw, they'd haul him out and string him up, too."

"If they had I bet he'd have told you where she is."

Russ shook his head. "I know a little bit more about hard-shells than you do, Will. They could have strangled him and he wouldn't have said a word. I didn't want a lot of killings, Will; lynching Enright would have stirred the squatters up against Bennett. After Bennett it would only be reasonable to hang every gunman."

"So you got the girl to help you."

"Not exactly. She volunteered to find maw. Now I'm gambling that she can do what I couldn't do—get her paw to give up; quit fighting and lay off the squatters—and bring maw back."

"What if she doesn't?"

Russ got up. "That's what's worrying me," he said.

Bill Metzen came up. "How's the wound, Russ?" he asked.

Will's eyes widened. "Did you get shot, Russ?"

"It's nothing. Some feller jumped out from between two buildings and let fly."

"Where?"

"Here," Russ said, touching his upper leg gingerly. "I'd better go down to the creek and wash it out."

"Russ . . . ?"

"I told you, Will, it's nothing. Don't worry about it." He turned and jerked his head at Metzen. The two of them walked away, towards the watercourse. While Russ bathed and inspected his injury Metzen sat with his back to a boulder, flipping pebbles into a ragged patch of shade.

"The boys're asking why you pulled out before you got your maw back, Russ."

"I'll tell you," Russ said. When he finished giving his reasons Metzen sighed and let his arms drop to his lap.

"I sure hope you're being smart," he said. "Why don't I ride out, hunt her up, and sort of tag along—just in case her paw makes trouble."

"It wouldn't work, Bill. In the first place there're still plenty of cowmen who'd shoot you on sight. In the second place—over fifty of us didn't cut it, so what good would one man do? And last—Forge Enright's a fighter; we could've killed him before he'd have told—but he loves his daughter. She could bring him around where all the guns in the country couldn't. I'm gambling on that. I was thinking that last night when I told her, in front of Forge—some of the doggoned things he and his people had done. I wanted her to be a little disillusioned, Bill, so that he'll have to work harder getting her respect back than he's ever worked fighting us."

"Use her against him, is that it?"

"I guess it is . . . Damn; this thing hurts."

"I reckon it does. Riding half the night didn't help

it any." Metzen twisted his head. " It doesn't look infected, though."

" There's no infection, I'll keep it clean so there won't be," Russ said. " Now I wish I'd knocked that bushwhacker in the head."

Metzen sloped his hat so the rising sun wouldn't strike his tired, red-rimmed eyes. " You can still do that, if you want to," he said.

Russ looked around. " Do you know who he was? "

" Yes; Mahoney talked to me about it. It was a squatter from south of Cornell named Hirsh;Dave Hirsh."

" I never saw the man before."

" He probably didn't know you either, except by sight and rumour, but for ten thousand dollars, a feller like Hirsh doesn't have to know someone to want to kill them."

Russ finished caring for the wound, went over into the shade near Metzen and sank down. " I'm bushed," he said.

" What about Hirsh. Any of the boys'll gladly ride down there tonight."

" Right now he isn't important. Let's get something to eat then sleep a while."

Metzen nodded, got up stiffly and brushed himself off. " And what if the girl don't make good? "

" We'll think about that this afternoon—after she's had her chance."

Down where the cooking fires were, men ate or sprawled in benign sleep. There were shadows across them, pointing up unshaven faces, sunken eyes, sweat encrusted clothes. In the background was the grunt and squeal of horses. The calls of sentries from time to time. He and Metzen ate in silence and later, sought different places to sleep.

The day before had been long and hot, the night which

had followed had been arduous and filled with uncertainty, things to drain the last of a man's energy. Lying there with the fragrance of the camp and spindly forest around him, Russ listened to the talk fall away until nothing remained, but the solid, slow tread of a sentry. His mind traced sluggishly the long pattern of his life. He thought also of the lives of those around him; of the ambitions, the opportunities, unfulfilled, and in most cases, no longer to be hoped for. Thought of the faces of their wives, thin from want, wan from fear and dread—ugly with anger. With clear insight—because he was a man and he knew other men were the same—he thought how it would be in years to come for these squatters. What they had done in the last fifteen hours would be warm to them the rest of their lives. Win or lose, being part of something momentous, even in this isolated country, would live in their memories as long as life held.

In times like this, when he was bone-weary, but could not find sleep, recollections crowded up vivid and sharp. He thought now as he had the past few years, of his father lying in the dark earth, dying and all relaxed; of the things his mother had said later; of the great, engulfing loneliness that had never left him and which still made him melancholy.

Then he thought of Diane Enright. He remembered the strike of her voice in the night. He saw the beseeching flash of her eyes and the touch of her hands. He recalled with extreme clarity how she looked in anger, when she was hating him with all her spirit, and how she looked along towards the last when she was fighting so desperately in her own way, to achieve ends she believed in.

That brought him back to the present; to the memory of Forge Enright's iron profile and to the uncertainty he felt over the older man's reactions. He had read it plainly in Enright's face, that he loved his daughter with a depthlessness. Now, would that be stronger than his hatred of squatters? If it was, the range war was over. If it wasn't . . .

He moved restlessly, finally sat up, made a cigarette, lit it, gazed around at the still camp and lay back again with smoke drifting straight up in a long spiral from his face.

The sun climbed steadily higher, hung directly overhead for an interminable time, then slanted off westerly and began a majestic descent, stalking gracefully across the brassy sky. Even in the shade it was sweat-hot. Outward and downward, where the prairie lay, dancing waves of heat distorted the scene farther than a man could see.

He turned up on his side and slept. Hours later, when thin, timid shadows were creeping from under brush and down along the eastern sides of the trees, someone shook him gently by the shoulder. He opened his eyes and peered upwards. Mahoney was squatting close.

" Some riders coming, Russ."

He struggled upwards and found that his wounded leg had a nagging pain in it that grew sharp and stabbing when he moved. " Who are they? "

" Don't know yet; anyway there's only four of them."

" Stragglers, probably," Russ said, probing the wound and finding it hot to the touch and more swollen.

" Uh, huh," Mahoney grunted. " Bill and I counted noses. These are strangers—at least they aren't any of our regular outfit."

" Better get some of the boys up and—"

" We've already got a welcoming committee waiting for 'em," Mahoney said. " Just thought we'd better wake you, that's all."

" Well—my leg's kind of sore. When they come in,

bring them over here, will you?"

"Sure," Mahoney said, and trudged back across the camp where other men were beginning to stir, to grumble and rub their limbs and scratch their heads. Someone was brewing fresh coffee, its aroma hung fragrantly in the heat.

Russ went to the creek, examined his wound, found it no worse than before, although more painful, then went over where his brother was. Will was sitting up, shirtless, shiny with bear-grease salve and looking better than he had since his branding. His eyes were questioning when Russ sat down gingerly.

"There's something going on," he said to Russ. "Some of your men caught their horses and rode down into the trees."

"I know. Some riders are coming."

Will's gaze swung swiftly southward, but his vision was obstructed by brush and trees. Words formed in his throat, but he didn't utter them.

Russ said, "We'll know soon enough," and rocked sideways to see his brother's back. The oldster who had been caring for the younger Morgan had done a professional job. The seared places were mending rapidly. There was no dryness to the skin anywhere. He rocked back again thinking with satisfaction of Henry Catlett's end.

The old man brought a tin plate for Will. When he saw Russ, he hesitated a moment with the plate and Russ stood up with a gesture towards his brother and walked away.

He was in his own shady spot when Mahoney came striding up, quirt dangling from his wrist. "They're here, Russ."

"Who are they?"

Mahoney took a big breath, as though relishing this moment. " The Enright girl, your mother, and a couple of riders."

" Fetch them; don't just stand there."

When they came there was a craggy sea of rough faces in the background. One gaunt, gangling man cleared his throat, spat aside and growled, " Leave 'em be, boys. Let's hustle some supper."

The crowd dispersed. Metzen and Mahoney lingered, watching. Russ was on his feet. His mother was smiling at him. There was something infinitely sad in her look that Russ found hard to face.

" How is Willy, Russ? "

" He's mending, maw."

" You've been hurt."

" Not enough to notice, hardly. I'm mostly stiff from sleeping on the ground." He turned. " Bill; take her to Will."

Diane Enright looked flushed and tired. He motioned towards the blanket on the ground and she dropped down upon it.

" I owe you a lot," he said. " I guess I owe you more than that, even." He sank down across from her and because he was nervous under her steady gaze, began twisting up a cigarette. When it was going he looked up. " How did you do it? "

She smoothed the blanket at her side as she spoke. " I offered to let any one of the men you locked in jail, out, if they would tell me where she was. Three of them accepted, but two of them just wanted to get out."

" The other one knew? "

" Yes, he knew. I rode over to Houton Creek and found her."

" He had her over there? " Russ said, incredulously.

She nodded. "Yes; some of your people were holding her. But that isn't important—not now."

"No, I guess it isn't, but I'm losing some of my faith in folks," he said slowly.

"Why; because there are squatters who would help cowmen?"

"Yes."

"What about cowmen who help squatters—like me?"

"That's different."

"No it isn't. Who you are doesn't make any difference when you're in trouble—it's the things you believe are right, that counts. There has been *some* friendliness between your people and mine. There always is *some* friendliness."

"Your father didn't try to stop you?"

"No," she replied slowly. "He left very shortly after you rode out of Cornell. I don't know where he went. I wanted to talk to him."

"I don't understand him," Russ said.

"No, I don't suppose you do. You two are too much alike."

"What I want to know—"

"Is whether he knows he is whipped," she finished for him. He nodded. "I know my father very well, and regardless of what you think of him, he's very dear to me, but he doesn't know how to take defeat." When he started to speak she broke in upon him. "Don't say anything against him for that. You're no different. But there is something else I want to tell you. Before I left for Houston Creek last night, I sent two Texas Company riders to Fort Davis."

He looked startled.

"Can you imagine what will happen if my father refuses to stop this fighting?"

He punched out the cigarette and said, " I see. You figured to call in the Army so that neither side could—"

" Exactly. Am I wrong? "

" I don't think it was necessary," he said. " I've got my mother back, Cornell is humbled a little, folks will come to their senses."

" I hope you're right. I hope with all my heart you're right—but if you aren't, Mister Morgan . . ."

" Sure, I understand. You sort of plan ahead, don't you; well, that's good sense, but it sure changes things —what you've done."

" In what way? "

" Many ways," he said thoughtfully. " If news gets around soldiers are coming, the gunhawks'll slope."

" There is nothing wrong with that."

" No; of course there isn't. But the squatters had better break up, too. Everybody better go home and lie low."

" That was in my mind," she said. " If you hadn't said it, I meant to."

He looked on her with irony. " I don't know as I ever knew a clever woman before," he said, " and I'm not sure I like meeting one now."

She leaned forward a little, her eyes alive with sincerity. " I'm not clever, I'm desperate. I was scared half to death last night. I'm still frightened. But, Mister Morgan—*someone* had to stop this before there was nothing left but dead people and a burnt town."

" Why didn't you tell me, before you called in the Army? "

" I thought of it. I also thought you would try to prevent it."

He caught the eye of a passing squatter and beckoned. When the man came closer he asked him to fetch Mahoney.

Diane watched him with apprehension, but when Mahoney came, and Russ spoke, it was about the outlaw they'd brought back from Cornell with them.

"How's he acting?"

"Well," Mahoney said a little ruefully, "if he has anything on his conscience it sure isn't interfering with his poker playing."

"Send him over."

Mahoney nodded and left. When Flake Willis strode up, he was wearing a careless little grin. He nodded to Diane and dropped down on the ground.

"You wanted me, Russ?"

"Yeh; Flake, the Army's coming." Russ watched the grin flicker out. "If we hold you until they come up it might be kind of uncomfortable for you."

"Well, now, Russ, I told you down in Cornell I didn't shoot no settlers. All I did—"

"I remember what you told me—only I haven't had time to check up on it."

"Well, it's true. I didn't bull you none at all. You ought to know me better'n that."

"I'd hate to hand you over to the soldiers."

"An' I'd hate having you hand me over to them, too," Flake said dryly. "Listen, Russ; consarn it, we did a lot of ridin' together."

"That's what I'm thinking of right now."

"Then take my word for what I told you."

Russ nodded. "All right, Flake, I'll take your word, but before you pull out I want you to do a couple of things for me."

"What?"

"You and I learned the trade in the same school. These people don't know the first thing about making a sashay around the countryside without being seen. I want you to take a ride down around Cornell, see if the soldiers've come up yet, then hunt up the cowmen, see what they're up to, and come back up here and let me know."

Willis removed his hat, scratched his awry head and replaced the hat. "I can find out about the cowmen all right. The Army might be a different thing."

"You don't have to take any chances," Russ said. "All I want to know is if they're in the country and if so, if they're sending out patrols—things like that."

"Why don't you just disband like we used to do? Lie low until the smoke's cleared away?"

"Because—if I disband, the squatters all head for home, and the cowmen are still riding in bands, they could hit every squatter-soddy for fifty miles before the squatters could reorganise and defend themselves."

"I see," Willis said. He got up. "All right. I'll report back as quick as I can." He half turned, then stopped. "You'd better tell Metzen and Mahoney I'm leaving."

Russ stood up, looked aside at Diane and said, "I'll be right back, wait here."

He found Mahoney and Metzen together, explained why he was releasing Flake Willis, and started back where Diane was. Old Man Lavender stopped him en route.

"Russ; some of the boys're rested enough and ready to ride again. They'd sort of like to know what you got in mind next."

"Tell them I'll be around shortly. Just relax for a while. If a few get restless, have them look after the horses." He walked away.

When Diane saw him coming she got up. "Your mother was looking for you," she said.

"Is something wrong?"

"No; she and I had a long talk while we were riding up here, Mister Morgan."

"I see. I think I understand, Miss Enright—and I'm perfectly willing to quit—but you can see my situation can't you?"

"Yes; I told her."

"And you approve?"

She nodded.

"Walk with me out along the rim," he said, and started to move away.

"It hurts you to walk, why don't we stay right here?"

"Naw, it doesn't hurt. The limp is for sympathy."

She smiled up at him and they went down among the trees to the drop-off. He used his hat to dust off a flat boulder for her and she sat down. Below was the shimmering panorama, a scene of heat-ridden country caught and frozen into a stillness. As far as either of them could see, there was no movement.

"It's big, isn't it, Miss Enright."

"A world to itself," she said.

He leaned against a lodgepole pine, relaxed in its shade. "Big enough for all the people in it and thousands more."

"Yes."

"For cowmen and squatters, and fences. Big enough so that folks who'll take a little time getting used to each other don't have to rub shoulders unless they want to."

She twisted to look up at him. "You don't have to convince me, Mister Morgan."

He sat down with his back to the tree, removed his hat and dropped it in the shade. "You didn't always think that way, though."

"I can't say exactly what I thought. You see, Mister Morgan, I went away to school when I was still small. When I came back I heard my father and others talk about squatters. I suppose you might say it was the environment. There were times when I didn't approve of things I heard about, but for every raid *we* made, I was told of the trespasses of the newcomers." She shrugged gently. " That morning I met you on the Houton Creek road—that was the first time I'd ever met a fighting squatter. The impression, you must admit, wasn't the kind to win sympathy and understanding. You told me of whipping a cowman and how you meant to whip others—my father included. Well; you may call it misplaced, Mister Morgan, but I was loyal to my own kind."

" You don't have to explain," he said. " The fact that you helped at all is better than a book full of explanations. I think—if you hadn't been in Cornell yesterday—things might have gone much different, Miss Enright. I'm not sure whether it was you, the wound, or just plain tiredness, but by yesterday evenin', I was ready to call quits."

" Maybe it was all three," she said, watching his face. " And maybe, like you said, I should've told you about the Army, but yesterday I wasn't sure I could trust you— completely, I mean. It seemed that I was alone, against my father and you, both."

" You can trust me," he said. " I'd give a lot of money to know about your paw, though. Our situation now is about like the kid sitting on the powder barrel. If he gets up it might explode, and if he doesn't get up, he'll starve. If we leave here, break up and go home—"

" Yes; I know. I wish I could tell you what my father might do. I wish there was some way to find out. I know him to be a stubborn and shrewd man, Mister Morgan."

" I sort of thought, with you pulling for an end to the thing, he might stop."

She looked at the hands in her lap. " Mister Morgan; a man doesn't lift himself from a saddle to partnership in one of the wealthiest cattle companies in the West by bending with sentiment. At least that's what I've been telling myself the last twenty hours."

" But what's dear to him—if you aren't? He has no other family."

" I'm dear to him, Mister Morgan. I'm probably the dearest thing in his life, but you're overlooking something; he knows I'm safe—with you or the cowmen."

Russ groped around for the tobacco sack, began making a cigarette with slow and meticulous attention. When it was going he exhaled deeply and gazed at her. " Diane," he said, " I've got a notion. It's pretty shocking, I reckon, but it looks like it'll take something like it to bring your paw around."

" What is it? " There was a soft shine to her face.

He didn't reply for a moment, then he said, " Let's wait until Flake Willis gets back, but I'll tell you this—you're the main actor in it."

His gaze held to her face in an unblinking way and she got up abruptly. " Let's go see your brother," she said.

Will Morgan was embarrassed when Diane Enright came up with Russ. He clutched the old blanket around his naked shoulders and smiled up at the girl. She knelt and persuaded him to show her his back. Russ went over where his mother was making a poultice of bruised sage leaves and grease. She looked as serene as he remembered her looking other times when she was occupied.

" She's a fine girl, Russ," his mother said. " A beautiful girl, too."

Russ looked at the ground and nodded without speaking.

" I want you to listen to her."

He got a twinkle in his eye. " I listen," he said lazily.

"I listen and look. Why is it that mothers—when the world's falling in—think of only one thing when they meet a nice girl and have an unmarried son?"

"Because they don't believe anything final will ever happen, son, nothing so disastrous that their boys can't be made to face it—overcome it—with a good woman to help them." She looked sideways at him. "You ought to go wash and shave; you're a sight."

"She hasn't run yet," he said.

"But she'd like it better if you cleaned up."

He smiled and turned back where Will was talking to Diane Enright. The girl's face was pale and her eyes large and dark looking. Will was minimising his injury in embarrassment. Russ said, "I'll be back directly," and left them.

At the creek he cleaned up as well as he could, but the razor in his saddlebag was dull. He was scraping away and wincing when Bill Metzen came up, watched for a moment then chuckled.

"First time I've seen you do that since we made this camp," he said. "Odd how a female or two'll change things, isn't it?"

"Not as odd as it is painful. Willis come back yet?"

"Naw; it's too early."

"Miss Enright sent riders for the Army, Bill."

"What!"

"Yeh. Go down and pass the word around for the boys to keep alert and have their saddles handy. Be sure the guards know they've got to keep a damned close watch. We don't want either the Army or the cowmen—if they're still feeling strong-heart—to slip up on us."

"Cowmen hell," Metzen exploded. "We better slope before the soldiers find us. There aren't very many of us they wouldn't make court-martial meat out of."

"That doesn't worry me much. Who'd be witnesses, Bill?"

"Are you crazy? The cowmen—who else?"

"And if the cowmen testified against us—what could we tell Uncle Sam about them?" When Metzen didn't reply, Russ said: "They hired outlaws to fight for them —we didn't. They've been burning and murdering for years—we haven't. No, Bill; I don't think there'll ever be any trials, but on the other hand I don't think we ought to let them slip on up us either, so make cussed sure those sentries are wide awake."

"*I* think," Metzen said with emphasis, "we ought to break up and go home, if we're likely to have a run-in with the Army. The boys'll think the—"

"Suppose Enright and Bennett aren't through night-riding; suppose they're out searching for squatters to kill right now? We've got to know what they're going to do before we do anything. Better to get captured by the Army like we are, then shot down one at a time at our soddies by renegade cowmen. Go pass the word, Bill. I'll be down when I'm through here."

He finished shaving, patted his face gingerly with cold creek water and stuffed the razor into his saddlebag, threw the pouches over his shoulder and went down where his saddlery lay. There he met Mahoney and several others, all excited. He told them everything he knew. There was a general discussion. The squatters finally agreed Russ's way was the best and went straggling off into the shadows, where the rest of the band was moving with uneasy restlessness.

Diane found him standing in the gloom, lost in thought. She smiled at him. "You look very presentable, Mister Morgan," she said. Then the little smile faded. "How could they have done that to your brother? He told me the name of the man who did it."

" Yes? "

" He told me you killed him, too."

" He should have let that stay buried."

" Oh, no; Mister Morgan—no. I would have done the same thing." She put a hand on his arm. He had something on his lips, but at her touch he left it unsaid.

" I don't know what to say—to believe. Did my father know that was going to be done? "

He started to shrug, then shook his head instead. " I don't think so. Your paw's hard, but I don't believe he'd torture a boy."

He reached up with his free hand, caught her fingers and held them. At that moment a voice sang out jarringly :

" Riders coming! "

CHAPTER 8

"*It's Your Show, Enright!*"

Diane stood up quickly and swung to see the roll of land below. Russ moved past her, also peering. He didn't see them at once. Behind them men were crashing through the underbrush, the clatter of their guns louder, even than their voices raised in excitement.

It was late afternoon with several hours of daylight still to come. Russ watched the riders without interference from reflected sunlight.

"Is it my father?" Diane Enright asked.

Russ shook his head. "I'm not sure yet. Too far off. I don't think it's the Army though; they aren't riding in ranks like soldiers do."

Bill Metzen came up, stood beside Russ without speaking, staring down the prairie. "Who led 'em here," he said, and answered himself. "That Willis feller, more'n likely."

Russ ignored the remark. "I'm more interested in who they are," he said.

Metzen turned to face him. "Cowmen—who else could they be?"

"It might be more squatters, or the Army. It might even be townsmen from Cornell or Houton Creek."

Metzen scowled. "They won't be friends, I don't think," he said, and resumed his study of the oncoming riders.

There were possibly twenty to thirty men in the cavalcade. They were loping steadily towards the squatters' stronghold. Pale daylight shone upon their metal equipment. They rode close, but in no particular order, and while the squatters watched, a solitary rider burst around the foot of the knoll and urged his horse upward with flailing motions of his spurred boots. Metzen let out a surprised curse.

"Who is *that*?" he said, not loudly and more to himself than to Russ and Diane.

Russ leaned out to peer at the frantic rider. "Why," he said, "that's Flake Willis. He must have been coming towards us from the east when he saw those riders."

"Well," Metzen observed with interest, "he's sure pushing his horse to stay ahead of them."

The edge of the knoll was crowded with squatters. They watched Willis force his horse up the trail leading to the top-out. From a long way off, several cat-calls echoed. Russ switched his attention to the distant group of riders. Several were brandishing carbines. He was satisfied about their identity and touched Metzen's arm.

"It's the cowmen, Bill. Go tell the boys to take cover and be ready, but not to fire until I give the word."

"Sure," Metzen said quickly. "I'll put some along the back trails up here, too." He squinted quickly, a little anxiously, at the sun. "I wish they'd showed up earlier—I don't care for fightin' in the dark."

"Go on. If you see Willis tell him where I am."

Metzen hurried away and Diane brushed Russ's arm with her finger. When he looked down at her he was astonished at the change in her expression. Her eyes were dark with dread, the soft lines of her mouth were drawn out nearly straight. He thought of what his mother had said of beauty, and thought that right then, Diane was not beautiful.

"Don't fight them," she said. "Please don't..."

"I won't. A little while ago I told you I had a notion. Well; I still have it. If that's your father I don't think he'll fight us either."

"Russ?"

He turned. Flake Willis, sweat-damp and flush-faced, was striding up.

"If you'd been a little later," Russ said, "they'd have had you, Flake."

The outlaw shot Diane a short glance and screwed up his face. "It was closer than I like, as it was."

"How come you didn't see them until you came around the hill?"

"See them! Hell, man; I've been watching them ever since they started up this way. I had to ride *around* them —had to cover two miles for every mile they covered. I seen them all right, and that ain't all I've seen, either."

" Is it Enright? " Russ asked.

Willis gave a curt headshake. " It's Bennett. That's why I hung around down there trying to figure things out. I thought Enright was king-bee of the cow outfits. I never did find him, but this Bennett—well sir—he's been riding all over hell's half-acre rounding up the boys who'll still fight for the cowmen."

" Bennett," Russ said, turning to look closer at the approaching riders. " I was planning on it being Enright."

" Well, un-plan, boy. It's Bennett of SB—I ought to know, I seen him plenty of times in Cornell."

" What else did you see, Flake? "

" Soldiers. I seen a whole herd of soldiers streaking it for Cornell. They're coming down from the northeast, Russ. Couple of columns of them. They're dragging a wheel-gun with them. It'll take them about two hours to get to Cornell. I figure it won't be hard for them to learn where Bennett and his crew are; some flannelmouth'll tell 'em—then they'll be coming up this way."

" Two hours," Russ mused.

" I ain't through yet," Willis said. " There's another bunch a-riding, too. Only about six or eight of 'em, but they've got the earmarks of some kind of a posse."

" Coming here? " Russ asked, with a puzzled frown.

" Yeh; heading this way from over by Houton Creek. I sort of guess them to be U.S. Marshals—or something like that. They aren't strong enough to do much unless they got a heap of law behind them."

" You couldn't get close enough to recognise any of these people, could you? "

Flake Willis gave Russ a dry stare. " I never tried," he said. " Now look, Russ; you said if I'd do this scouting for you I could ride on. Well; I don't aim to hang around here much longer, pardner, because there's going to be a hell of a mess start working pretty quick now, and the Army's bad enough—but if those other fellers are U.S. lawmen—why I just naturally got no hankering to swap lies with 'em. All right?"

"All right, Flake," Russ said, and stuck out his hand. "Good luck, old timer. If you see any of the boys up around Virginia Dale, say hello for me."

Flake shook Russ's hand quickly, mumbled something, spun on his heel and hastened off.

Diane's colour had returned. There were two vertical lines just above her eyebrows. "I don't understand," she said. "Where is my father—if he isn't leading the cowmen?"

A gunshot exploded down on the prairie before Russ could reply. He motioned for Diane to move back from the rim and took several backward steps himself.

The cowmen were fanning out. Some apparently had received previous orders to flank the knoll. Their cries came musically to the men atop the hill, watching them.

Mahoney came up with a grim look on his face. "Bill's got the back trails covered pretty well, Russ. I got the front country fixed so's they'll sure wish they hadn't—if they attempt to storm up here. I met Willis ridin' easterly through the trees. He said you'd told him to beat it."

"I did," Russ said, and recited what Flake had told him. "I wish to hell we had Enright to deal with instead of Bennett."

Mahoney glanced at the line of cowmen halting down below, just beyond gun-range. His stance indicated that it made no difference to him which cowman they had to fight, if they had to fight any at all. He said nothing.

Diane took several steps forward when one of the men

down below began to call out. She listened to the man a moment, then said: " That's Saul Bennett."

Russ nodded, listening to Bennett, who was yelling to the squatters, and when the cowman finished, he called out: " Save your breath, Bennett. You aren't coming up here and we aren't putting down our guns."

" We'll be up," Bennett shouted. " We'll be up when it gets dark in another hour or two, Morgan. If you're smart—"

" Where's your pardner, Bennett? Where's Forge Enright? You'll need him to run things before this is over. Where is he?"

Bennett made no reply to the question, instead he warned the squatters what would happen if they didn't come down off the hill with their hands high. This was greeted with several derisive shouts and Metzen turned to Russ Morgan.

" Do you reckon that damned fool doesn't know the soldiers are at Cornell?"

" I know he doesn't," Russ replied. " If he did he wouldn't be wasting time trying to smoke us off here, and those fools with him would be lighting a shuck out of the country as fast as they could."

Metzen returned to his study of the cowmen a moment, then he began walking away, over towards the scalloped edging of rock where several squatters were hunkered.

" The notion you mentioned," Diane said quietly, without finishing it.

Russ moved his feet, stood hip-shot watching the cowmen assign horse-holders, draw out their carbines and assemble near Saul Bennett. " It's no good," he said, " unless your paw's here."

A tentative burst of gunfire directed upwards, came from the cowmen. Mahoney came trotting up with a worried look.

"Russ; there's more riders coming." Mahoney gestured with an out-flung arm to indicate the northeast.

"Very many?"

"'Can't tell yet. It don't look like more'n a handful, but there might be more scattered out." Mahoney looked at the fish-belly sky with anxiety. "I got no liking for this," he added.

Russ said, "Put a man with strong eyes on the highest ridge, Mahoney, and have him report to me as soon as he sees any other riders coming."

"Others," Mahoney said. "Hell's bells; do you expect still more?" He fidgetted. "I wish we'd took down off of here while we still had the chance." When Russ made no reply, Mahoney stalked away.

"Russ...?"

He swung quickly, took her arms and pulled her back off the rim. "Go stay with my mother and Will. Don't get near the edge of the hill and don't let them get near it either. As soon as I can I'll come see you." He gave her a slight push away, and started across the deserted camp.

Bill Metzen's face glistened with sweat when he swung it towards Russ. "Now what?" he asked. "Bennett wasn't bluffing; they're going to try to come up here."

"It looks that way. Pick about ten good shots and have them lay a little lead in front of Bennett's boys. Don't shoot to hit, though; plenty of time for that later."

Metzen nodded and moved off among the brush and trees. Old Burt Lavender quirked a sly look at Russ and spat into the dust at his feet. "I could put a ball right between Bennett's feet, if ye'd like," he said.

Russ looked at the handsome old musket in Lavender's hands and thought it likely the old man could do exactly that. He said, " Go ahead."

Lavender stretched out his lean, stringy body, snugged the Pennsylvania rifle to his cheek and lowered his head over it fondly. For a second not a muscle moved the full length of his body; even his rib-cage stopped moving. There was a sharp explosion, clean and high-pitched, followed by a wisp of dirty smoke, and Lavender raised his head a fraction to peer downwards. Saul Bennett, in startlement, had leapt backwards, crashed over a niggerhead boulder and fallen into the wiry, spined limbs of a grey chapparral bush. He began threshing and cursing in an effort to get clear of the chapparral. In that moment Russ held his breath. He thought Bennett had been hit.

A peal of laughter lifted from the places where squatters crouched when several cowboys helped Bennett get to his feet. The cowman swore a mighty string of oaths and glared upwards. Old Man Lavender quirked his head at Russ. There was a satisfied twinkle in his eye.

" He ne'er thought they'd be a musket up here could reach any further'n a carbine, did he? "

Russ smiled and shook his head without replying.

The cowmen seemed to find a dozen reasons for hesitating after Lavender's shot. They were still milling around when Metzen's riflemen fired a ragged volley downwards. While Russ watched, an argument of some kind broke out among them. This was also evident to many of the squatters. They began calling down in a tantalising way, teasing the cowboys, daring them to try and ascend the hill.

Mahoney came up with a carbine in his fist. " Russ," he said, " those riders from over Houton Creek way are pretty close now. Still looks like only a half dozen or so. They're making right for the hill."

" Close enough to recognise yet? "

" No; what do you want us to do about them? "

"If they get too close turn them back with a few shots. Willis said he saw them hours ago. He thought they were lawmen."

"They might be," Mahoney replied, "but badges aren't going to do 'em much good—with that mob out on the prairie."

"I wouldn't make any bets on that, Mahoney. Bennett's got some lads with him that'll slope as soon as lawmen appear. I'm only surprised Bennett was able to round up as many gunmen as he did. I thought sure most of the killers would pull out, after what we did to their town last night."

"I recognised a few of the fellers he's got with him and they're just cow outfit riders, not gunmen. I expect the real gunmen did pull out, and Bennett's gone and rounded up the riders in a final effort to smash us."

"If that's so, I don't think we've got a whole lot to worry about. There won't be many cowboys down there who'll like the idea of storming this hill."

It was obvious to the watchers this was exactly what was happening. After Bennett's close call, several of his crew were very much opposed to climbing the hill while daylight lasted. The longer Bennett's riders talked and argued, the more adherents one faction recruited, until Bennett finally threw up his arms and turned away from them. It then became obvious which faction had triumphed, for all the riders moved back out where the horses were being tended, and squatted down to smoke and talk while watching the hilltop one moment, the slow and gradual descent of the sun, the next moment.

Satisfied, Russ motioned for Mahoney to lead the way, and followed the smaller man across the campground to the rear slope, where men stood around in the dark shade of pines, watching horsemen approach from the northeast.

It was cooler on that side of the hilltop. The late afternoon sun didn't strike there; the pines exuded a strong aroma and except for the attention rivetted upon the little band of riders sweeping closer, the squatters seemed unruffled and unworried.

"There," Mahoney said, pointing, and almost instantly Russ had a premonition. He walked out into plain sight and began to make a cigarette. When the match flared, Mahoney came up beside him.

"If they're lawmen we ought to haze them around the hill. Bennett's boys'd get the surprise of their lousy lives if the U.S. Marshal rode up now."

"They aren't lawmen," Russ said, watching the riders over his cigarette. They're cowmen. See that ramrod-straight feller out front; that's Forge Enright."

"Enright..." Mahoney said, with rising inflection. "How come him not to be with Bennett?"

"I don't know and I don't care, but I'm glad to see him show up here."

"Glad!"

Russ got up, worked his leg a little and went over into the shade. "Yeh; glad. Now do like I tell you. When they're almost within range let 'em have a round or two. The men around the hill will hear and come riding to see what's going on. That way Bennett and Enright'll meet —if they didn't expect to see each other out here. I think they'll all go around to the prairie side. If they do, let me know right away. Understand?"

"I understand," Mahoney said. "You got an idea."

Russ went to the little glen where his brother, mother, and Diane were. Will had a carbine leaning beside him against a boulder. His face was alive with clear vitality. It was apparent to Russ the women were having trouble keeping Will from joining the others. He frowned at his brother, stopping the words before they came.

"You just sit back down there and take it easy," he said. When Will would have protested he gazed darkly at him in silence. Will subsided.

Diane asked a question. He told her he was certain her father was approaching from the direction of Houton Creek and she frowned thoughtfully.

"You don't suppose he rode over there trying to stop me from getting to your mother, do you?"

Russ wagged his head. "You said he left Cornell before you did. If that's so, he had plenty of time to beat you to the draw on that."

"Did you keep them from starting a fight?" she asked.

"*I* didn't. Seems Bennett's boys aren't anxious to storm this hill. One of our men dropped a slug right under Bennett. His riders cooled off real quick after that."

"Are they quitting, then?"

"Naw; we aren't that lucky. But I don't think they'll try anything until after dark. Meanwhile, I've still got that notion. Now that your paw's here, we may be able to try it out."

"You said I was involved in that."

"You are. You won't like your part, but it can't be helped."

She regarded him with curiosity, but since he volunteered nothing more, she refrained from probing. Russ's mother moved over behind her younger son with the pan of salve. She spoke to Russ while putting a fresh layer of grease on Will.

"Do you think you can hold them off until the Army gets out here?"

"By the time the Army gets here," Russ said dryly, "I hope we're all long gone. There's no telling what Enright and Bennett'll do if the soldiers come up on them in the dark, and I don't want to be anywhere near if there's shooting between civilians and soldiers."

A muted ripple of gunfire caused Diane to start up. Russ saw fear shade her face, and touched her with his fingers. When she faced him he said, " It's a signal; nothing to worry about. Now you three stay right here." He bent a look upon his brother. " That means you, especially. Don't leave this spot."

He limped down where Bill Metzen and most of Morgan's Men were crouched low, listening to the shouts of the riders down below. Metzen appeared more quizzical than apprehensive. Russ explained about his instructions to Mahoney, while watching several of Bennett's men mount up, whirl and dash around the base of the hill.

Moments later the group of riders with Forge Enright swept into sight easterly and southerly of Russ Morgan's vantage point and reined up in a sliding halt at sight of Bennett's men. Several men called out at once and Bennett himself loped up. For several minutes a parley was undertaken where they met, the both groups turned and rode slowly back towards Bennett's bivouac. In the lead, Enright and Bennett were engrossed in conversation. From time to time, Russ could see Enright turn and gaze upwards.

For a while there was little to see so far as the cowmen's camp was concerned, then, just as Mahoney came out of the trees and underbrush near Russ, the cowmen began to stir themselves.

" Russ; I sent a couple of the boys down to sort of take a look around, in case those fellows with Enright've got pardners hid out behind us somewhere."

" That was pretty risky," Russ said.

" Be a sight riskier if Enright brought a crew back to slip up on us."

"I guess so. Keep a sharp watch back there." He raised his head and called for Metzen. When the shorter man came up and Mahoney started off, Russ said: "Enright's going to make them do what Bennett couldn't ... Look!"

The cowmen were mounting. Forge Enright was sitting his horse slightly apart. When Bennett rode up to him and spoke, Enright fired a curt response. Bennett lapsed into silence and watched the cowboys get ready for the assault.

Metzen said, "We'd better throw up a little dust in front of them again, Russ."

"Go get Diane. Tell her to hurry up here."

The cowmen were ranged out for a solid assault. Russ was impressed that Forge Enright could make them do what both common sense and Saul Bennet had indicated was extremely unwise. He watched them approach the fringe of rifle range at a walk. Past that—there were very few rifles among the squatters—they rode steadily until within carbine range. By then the squatters were crouching over, tense and watching. There wasn't a sound.

Russ heard the swish of Diane's dress before he turned. She swept past him a little way and stared at the horsemen. Russ spoke aside to Bill Metzen.

"Get a lariat, Bill. See that tree near the rim—the one with the limb sticking out?"

"Yes."

"Wait for me over there."

Diane turned. There was the dark overtone to her gaze. "Russ; it's my father. He's leading them up here."

"I know. Come on; I've got a notion that'll stop him. If he's stopped the others'll quit."

They went over near the gnarled old tree where Bill Metzen was standing with a coil of rope in his hand.

Russ motioned overhead.

"Toss it over the limb, Bill."

Down below the horsemen could see them plainly, Their faces were upturned. Most of them had either carbines or pistols in their hands.

"Make a hangman's noose."

Metzen held the rope and stared at Russ in astonishment. "What?" he said.

"Hurry up, dammit; make a hangman's noose."

But Metzen didn't hurry. His astonishment passed and a stubborn anger replaced it. "Russ; you don't—"

"Give me that rope!"

Russ began making the loops, twisting and knotting until he'd fashioned a noose. When he held it up to see that it was right, a ring of men's faces were in the background. There was utter stillness. He moved over beside Diane, held the hangman's noose high and waved it. The cattlemen were watching. Several reined up dumbfounded.

"Enright!"

The cowman slowed but did not stop. He was staring upwards. When he saw the girl beside Russ, he pulled back sharply on the reins. His horse stopped and threw its head. Enright was squinting with his head on one side.

"Diane? Is that you, Diane?"

"Yes; it's me."

Enright froze. For a long electric moment there wasn't a sound, then: "Morgan; set her loose."

"I reckon not," Russ said. "You started this business of using women as hostages."

"I don't have your mother any more, Morgan. Diane got her—she should be up there with you right now."

"She is. That's not what I'm talking about, Enright. I've got your daughter. It's up to you what happens now."

"I told you what I'd do to you if you touched her, Morgan."

"Kill me? I don't think you're man enough, Enright, but if you are—will that bring her back?"

"You wouldn't dare. Why; they'd—"

"You thought that about Cornell too, didn't you? If you doubt what I'd do to her just lift your reins; just start riding up here." Russ turned and spoke quickly to Metzen. "Tighten the rope a little—take the slack up." He bent a little and placed the noose around Diane's throat. She was ashen, but her gaze was steady.

"Was this the notion you said I wouldn't like to take part in?"

"Yes. I'm bluffing Diane—you know that. Just pray it works ... Pray it works."

Metzen drew in the slack and Diane put up a hand to keep the noose from scratching her neck. Down below, an agitated cowboy let off an oath. Now all the squatters were standing up, forgetful of concealment or the fact that their enemies were well within carbine range. It was so still, Enright's voice carried with bell-like distinctness.

"Take that rope off my daughter, Morgan!"

"Sure; the minute you toss that pistol in your hand down and tell those other fellows to do the same thing."

Saul Bennett leaned from the saddle and said something to Enright. The older man listened without taking his eyes off Diane. He spoke sharply and swiftly aside. Bennett straightened up and said no more.

"Morgan—take that rope off her!"

Russ could feel sweat running under his shirt. His throat was dry and the tongue in his mouth was like wood. Instead of answering, he took Diane by the shoulders and led her over under the limb. "Take up the rest of the slack," he said to Metzen. When the rope drew up gently, Diane looked into Russ's face.

"I'm praying," she said. "If my prayers aren't answered I almost hope you will hang me."

He looked pale and unpleasant. "Don't be silly," he said. "If anyone had to hang it'd be me, not you. Me and your paw—damn his black old heart."

"Maybe I could say something to—"

"No; you're scared. You think I'm going to hang you and you're scared to death."

He finished adjusting the rope and turned. The cowmen were like statues. Forge Enright's pistol lay in his lap. The fist holding his reins was clenched until the bones showed through to those around him.

"All right, Enright; we're ready to fight you. There're more squatters up here than you've been able to collect from the cow outfits. But before we wipe you out, your daughter'll be swinging from that limb. You want to make folks suffer—well—try a little of it on your own soul for a change. Now—either toss that gun down or start praying. You haven't got long to make up your mind."

Enright was staring hypnotically at his daughter. "Diane? Honey are you all right?"

Russ hissed at her without looking. "Cry; break down and cry."

But she didn't. She nodded her head up and down so that her father could see, but she didn't speak a word.

"Good God Almighty," a cowboy yelped suddenly. "You can't let 'em hang your daughter, Mister Enright. Hey, fellers; we can't sit here an'—"

"Shut up you!"

Under Enright's savagery the cowboy subsided, but his bulging eyes and open mouth continued to indicate how appalled he was. Some of the other riders began to fidget in their saddles.

Russ called out: " It's your show, Enright. The time's up. Throw down that gun or start riding up here. I don't give a damn which you do."

Quite unexpectedly, Saul Bennett spoke out. " Let her go, Morgan. We'll give you that twenty-thousand to let her go."

" You fool," Enright raged at him. " You total damned idiot; that man Morgan doesn't care for money. Can't you get that through your fat skull! "

Russ spoke softly. " Bill; lead up a saddled horse." When the animal was procured, he gestured. " Put her in the saddle. Fine. Now Bill—hold tight to the bridle; whatever you do don't let that horse jump out from under her."

" The rope's not tied at the other end," Metzen assured him, but he grasped the cheek-piece and reins just the same.

Russ moved closer to Diane, reached up to adjust the rope. " Please don't hate me for using you like this," he said.

" I'm praying for you, Russ. It's got to work."

" Morgan! " Enright was sitting bolt upright in the saddle. " Morgan! Take that rope off her. I'll talk terms, but you take that rope off her."

Russ shook his head. Sweat was running down his forehead, half-blinding him with its saltiness. " *You aren't talking terms, Enright, I am. For the last time— throw down that gun in your hand and tell those other fellers to toss theirs down!* "

Tension mounted. Off to the west the sun touched a mountain snag and seemed to burst like egg-yolk, flooding the land with its last red glows.

Forge Enright lifted the gun in his lap, held it out between he and Saul Bennett, and dropped it. The sound of its landing upon the baked earth was audible. Without waiting, the cowboys dropped their guns also. Saul Bennett reached down to his holster and let the gun there fall.

"Now take that rope off her."

Russ turned, reached up for the rope and encountered Diane's hands. Her fingernails bit down deep into the palms of his hands. There was a mistiness to her gaze. The rope fell away.

"Now ride up, Enright. Lead those fellows with you and take it slow."

They filed up. The squatters met them, took their horses as they debouched atop the knoll and herded the unarmed men together. Forge Enright, pale and with an expression as lowering as thunder, walked over where Diane was standing beside Russ. Burt Lavender chuckled at him, leaning upon his Pennsylvania rifle, chewing tobacco slowly and with relish.

Before Enright could speak, Russ said, "There's one last thing, Enright. That twenty-thousand you're so all-fired anxious to be rid of—you're going to donate that in cash to a squatter's-fund. You and Bennett."

"Am I?" the old cowman said in an icy tone.

"I think you will, and I think you'd better hurry up and agree."

"Why should I agree—or hurry either?"

"Because the Army's on its way up here by now and I don't think you want to be taken by them, attacking a bunch of squatters."

"You're lying."

Russ looked over at Diane. The girl inclined her head at Forge Enright. "That's right, dad. I sent for the Army. Russ's had a scout watching for them. He saw them going towards Cornell with field guns. By now they're probably on their way here. It wouldn't be hard to find out where you and Mister Bennett are."

" *You* sent for the Army, Diane? "

" Yes."

" She did it to save your hide—and mine," Russ said " Are you going to agree to donate the twenty thousand or not? "

" If I refuse? "

" Why, then," Russ said, " I'll ask every squatter who has ever been burnt out or whipped or shot at, to take his story to the soldiers. We'll all unite in testifying against you and your riders."

Saul Bennett looked badly frightened. He moved forward until he was beside Enright. " Go ahead, Forge, dammit; give them the money." He looked over at Russ. " I'll take that reward off you, Morgan. I'll give you my word on that."

Russ flickered a glance over the lesser man, then resumed his duel with Diane's father. " Hurry up, Enright, we haven't got all night."

" Twenty thousand," Enright said dully. " You've got my word on it." With sarcasm he then said: " Anything else you sod-busters want, Morgan? "

" There is something else, yes, but I don't want it when you're in this mood. Someday I want your word you'll give the squatters a chance."

Enright swung to look at his daughter. " Are you all right, honey? "

" Yes; Oh dad; I didn't *want* to go against you. I never did anything so hard before in my life."

Enright cleared his throat. " Don't make a spectacle of your emotions in front of these people," he said. " We can talk later." He turned, gazed at Bennett a moment. " Half of that twenty thousand'll have to come out of you, Saul."

"I'll give it."

Enright looked farther back, where his unarmed riders stood. "You fellers; get your horses and get out of here. Don't ride towards Cornell. Scatter out and go home separately. If you see soldiers—don't let them catch you. Now ride!"

The squatters moved aside to let the cowboys leave. Several of them caught up their own horses and stood uncertainly beside them watching Russ. Bill Metzen got close to Russ.

"What about us?" he said.

"Same thing, Bill. Head for home, all of you. Say nothing to anybody—least of all the soldiers. You'd better make tracks."

It required no additional urging to send the squatters after their horses and down the trail from atop the knoll. When only the three Morgans and the two Enright's remained, with Saul Bennett fidgetting beside his own horse, Russ erected a cigarette and jerked his head at Bennett.

"You too. Hit the saddle and keep going."

They listened to the diminishing hoof-falls until the last one had faded away. Enright filled his pipe, lit it and puffed up a strong head of smoke. There was a look of dark iron in his gaze.

"Diane, honey; what I did—was it so wrong?"

"I don't want to know how much of it you knew about, dad," she replied gently. "I know why you did it—I understand. Can't we just let it die like that? There won't be any more."

"No," Forge Enright said, "there won't be any more."

"You're a hard man to convince," Russ said. "You should've been convinced after Cornell."

"Humph! Because some silly idiots on work horses

came in and took over for a few hours? I never figured that was a lasting threat, Morgan. Except that you had Diane with a rope around her neck, I'd have swept the whole lot of you off this hill."

"That was pure bluff."

"I thought it was," Enright said, "but would you call a man's bluff when he was fixing to lynch your only daughter?"

"I guess I wouldn't," Russ said.

Diane spoke again. "You two have made your war and I've asked nothing much of either of you so far, for my small part in it. Now I want to ask you both to do something for me." She paused, looked into their faces a moment. "For *my* sake—not for the squatters or the cowmen, but just for me—please shake hands."

Russ's mother moved in closer. Behind her, Will, with a shirt over his shoulders, strained to see their faces in the darkening night.

"Dad? Russ? For me—won't you do it?"

Russ moved first. There was no graciousness in the way he offered his huge paw, but there was even less willingness in the way Forge Enright's fist darted out, grasped the larger man's fingers fleetingly and drew back quickly to his side.

Diane sighed; she was so close to Russ he could feel her fingers near his. In the gloom he groped for them, found them and pressed his fingers tightly for a space. She returned the pressure.

"We'd better get away from here," Russ said finally, "but I'd like to ask one question, Mister Enright, before we split up. How come you weren't with Bennett when he came out to make his fight?"

"Remember, I heard Diane say she was going to find your mother and release her. Well; I rode over to

Houton Creek to do it before she got there."

"But why? You refused to do it last night in Cornell."

"Well; but I was being forced, don't you see. The other way I was doing it because I wanted to. You were right, Morgan; I knew it last night after the way I saw you were fighting us. Not like In'ians. Like white men fight. It wasn't right of me to take your mother hostage. I hurried over to set her free."

"Well; but you left town before Diane did—why didn't you get to Houton Creek first?"

"I got waylaid by some of the hired gunmen. They made me go back to Cornell with 'em and get their pay from the Company's safe. They pulled out, you see, and that held me up an hour. By the time I finally did get to Houton Creek..."

"Diane had already been there—released my mother and was fetching her here."

"Yes. Now let's get away from here." Enright turned to Mrs. Morgan with a stiff little bow. "I'd be proud, ma'm, if you'd accept the hospitality of my home, at least until tomorrow, when you could make the further journey to your own place. I'm thinking about the boy there—and his hurt."

Mrs. Morgan declined with dignity and without smiling, until, past the whipcord figure of Enright, she saw the wistful gaze of his daughter, then she relented.

They began the descent shortly afterwards, Forge Enright riding in the lead, Will Morgan behind him. Mrs. Morgan following the silhouette of her younger son, and farther back, where the darkness lay in velvet layers, Russ and Diane Enright rode side by side, content to be that close without speaking.

The End

Lauran Paine who, under his own name and various pseudonyms has written over 900 books, was born in Duluth, Minnesota, a descendant of the Revolutionary War patriot and author, Thomas Paine. His family moved to California when he was at an early age and his apprenticeship as a Western writer came about through the years he spent in the livestock trade, rodeos, and even motion pictures where he served as an extra because of his expert horsemanship in several films starring movie cowboy Johnny Mack Brown. In the late 1930s, Paine trapped wild horses in Northern Arizona and even, for a time, worked as a professional farrier. Paine came to know the Old West through the eyes of many who had been born in the previous century and he learned that Western life had been very different from the way it was portrayed on the screen. "I knew men who had killed other men," he later recalled. "But they were the exceptions. Prior to and during the Depression, people were just too busy eking out an existence to indulge in Saturday-night brawls." He served in the U.S. Navy in the Second World War and began writing for Western pulp magazines following his discharge. It is interesting to note that all of his earliest novels (written under his own name and the pseudonym Mark Carrel) were published in the British market and he soon had as strong a following in that country as in the United States. Paine's Western fiction is characterized by strong plots, authenticity, an apparently effortless ability to construct situation and character, and a preference for building his stories upon a solid foundation of historical fact. *Adobe Empire* (1956), one of his best novels, is a fictionalized account of the last twenty years in the life of trader William Bent and, in an off-trail way, has a melancholy, bittersweet texture that is not easily forgotten. *Moon Prairie* (1950), first published in the United States in 1994, is a memorable story set during the mountain man period of the frontier. In later novels such as *The Homesteaders* (1986) or *The Open Range Men* (1990), he showed that the special magic and power of his stories and characters had only matured along with his basic themes of changing times, changing attitudes, learning from experience, respecting nature, and the yearning for a simpler, more moderate way of life. His most recent Western novels include *Tears of the Heart, Lockwood* and *The White Bird*.